# RETURN
## TO
# AUSCHWITZ

### By

## KEVIN PAUL
# WOODROW

# RETURN TO AUSCHWITZ

# Return to Auschwitz

This work is based on a story told to me by
Holocaust survivor

## Krystyna Tsisaruk

Names have been changed to protect the
memories of the families and loved ones of those who
did not survive.

May they Rest in Peace

# DEDICATION

This Book Is Dedicated To
My Wonderful Friend

## Irmi Eichner
## XXX

Thank you for all your help

# CONTENTS

# CHAPTER 1
# THE ARRIVAL

The train suddenly jolted to a halt with its occupants being scattered everywhere. Peter Florea heard the doors being slid open, along with the commotion and crescendo of the noise that followed.

"Everybody out – Schnell - Schnell – quickly – out of the train," an excited voice was heard to scream over and over again, accompanied by the sound of many vicious dogs barking angrily. Peter wondered what the German handlers had done to these dogs to make them hate the new arrivals almost as much as the human guards did.

Although feeling extremely nervous, he was glad the journey had finally ended and he was able to stretch out and breathe fresh air again, but he was not expecting the sights, sounds and smells which greeted him.

He stayed in his corner position of the cattle truck for as long as he could, in an effort to prolong his final moments of relative freedom before becoming the sole property of the Nazis.

Those who were able to slowly exited the cattle truck but made slow progress, despite constantly receiving abuse and being shouted at by the German officers.

"Schnell – Schnell - Schnell!" they kept demanding.

The truth was they were just too tired to rush. Many were also too old or feeble, as well as being far too weak after the long journey to negotiate the four foot drop from the exit to the waiting ground below.

The people who had severe trouble leaving the transport were welcomed with a resounding beating by one or more of the many waiting guards!

As the compartment, his home for the past two days became more and more empty; Peter was able to take a closer look around the truck. This was a space usually occupied by ten to fifteen head of cattle, but for the past two days, had been occupied by at least one hundred and fifty people, supplied with no water and just two buckets to relieve themselves in. These buckets, he observed had been filled and then knocked over countless times during this journey to Hell!

Looking around the structure, Peter noticed the floor was now covered in urine and faeces. He also noticed that sadly not all of the prisoners had made it. There were at least twenty dead bodies lying strewn across the floor.

He panicked as he saw someone's hands placed on the floor of the entrance, and then pull his body inside the compartment. He watched as this young man emerged and began searching through the bodies. He was dressed in clothing that looked like striped pyjamas, whilst strangely wearing a Russian Army coat. The young man almost froze as he spotted Peter in the corner.

"Who are you, and why are you still in here?" the surprised young man questioned Peter. Without receiving an answer, he tried again. "You cannot be here. If they find you hiding in this truck, your life will be over. What is your name?" the young man asked again.

"It's Peter, Peter Florea," Peter replied.

"And how old are you, Peter," the strangely dressed man enquired.

"I am sixteen, Sir," he confirmed.

"Don't call me Sir, my name is William," the inquisitor told him a little angrily. "I am NOT one of those monsters!"

"Sorry," Peter said sheepishly.

"I like you, Peter," William said. "I will try my best to help you."

"Thank you, um, er, William," Peter said.

"Peter, you must never call me by name when a guard or officer can hear you," William informed the lad. "It wouldn't be good for either of us."

"Sorry," Peter said again.

"Now, when you get outside you must quickly blend in with the rest of the arrivals. You will be questioned about your age and if you have any skills. You must tell them you are eighteen years of age and you are an engineer."

"But I don't know anything about engineering or being an engineer," Peter pleaded.

"That doesn't matter," William said. "The chances are you will never see the officer again, or more to the point, he will see so many people tonight that he will not remember you. If they think you are intelligent, and so useful to the SS, there is a good chance you will survive the night and wake in the morning."

"My, oh my, is it really that bad in here?" Peter queried.

"My friend, I can honestly tell you that you will never have seen anything like this, nor been anywhere as bad as this before in your life!" William stated. "Welcome to Hell!" he added before suggesting, "Now let's attempt to get you safely off this thing."

He went to the exit and gestured to another young man to help. The other man who was about the same age as William, which Peter guessed would be around eighteen or nineteen, joined them. He looked suspiciously at Peter.

"No time to explain," William told his co-worker. "Just help me get him off." The two picked up one of the bodies from the floor and began dragging it to the exit. "Get behind me," William ordered the now even more nervous Peter, who did as was told.

When the three had reached the frame of the door, William and his co-conspirator jumped down and formed a barrier, a human shield for Peter to hide behind as he climbed down from the cattle truck.

"Good luck, Peter. May God be with you," William said, before gesturing for the young lad to blend in with the rest of the arrivals. "I will try and find you tomorrow." This was his parting gesture, as he patted the youngster on the back.

If young Pater thought the train smelled bad, it was nothing compared to the stench attacking his nostrils now. The scene was pure chaos! The guards were seemingly picking out the old and infirm to attack, striking them over and over again with their rifle butts, for no apparent reason whatsoever. To Peter, it looked like it was some kind of sport for the guards. More worryingly, they were laughing and they all seemed to be enjoying hurting these people!

The young lad took a quick look around at his new surroundings, observing that the air was filled with constant black smoke billowing from the four chimneys, which he could see in the distance. This gave a putrid, acrid odour to the air, as these chimneys belched putrid gasses into the cool night sky.

'What in earth are they burning?' Peter questioned himself.

He noticed an SS officer was looking at the people with total contempt, with obviously not an ounce of compassion in his bones. As the queue approached the officer, he looked at them and told them to join the line to the left, or the queue to the right. Peter noted that those who went to the right were mainly old men and women, or young mothers with children.

He thought that maybe they had a special place where the elderly could relax, whilst the mothers and children could play in a special area, maybe an area where these children could play, with swings, roundabouts and slides for them to enjoy. How wrong could he have been in this assumption!

He saw a young family split up by the officer. He waved the husband to join the queue to go to the left, but told his wife and child to go to the right. The young mother became hysterical and fell to her knees sobbing.

"I want to stay with my husband," she cried frantically.

"You insolent Jewess, take the child," the officer ordered one of the guards, who then tried to wrench the baby from the mother's arms.

"No – Please don't take my baby," she shouted. "He's done nothing to you. He's just an innocent child."

As the guard finally took the screaming baby away from the now grieving mother, her parting words to the officer were, "You are all monsters! I hope you all rot in Hell."

Hearing the woman say this, the SS officer unfastened the clasp on his holster, took out the luger contained within it and shot the mother clean between the eyes.

"Clean this up," he gave the order to William and his co-worker, Claus.

'So this is what they do,' Peter thought to himself, as he watched all these events taking place with horror.

Following orders, William and Claus picked up the dead woman and threw her unceremoniously into a wheeled container, where other bodies of the people who'd not survived the journey already lay.

Peter wondered what would happen to the child, the poor thing was only maybe six months old if it was a day. This question was answered immediately, when he heard the officer in charge give the order to William and Claus.

"And throw the baby in the cart also. It would not survive without the mother's tit anyway." Some of the guards began laughing when they heard this.

Peter couldn't believe this man's arrogance. He didn't even know the sex of the baby but was killing it anyway.

Eventually, Peter reached the murderer and it was his turn to receive questioning. He had to try very hard to hide his contempt for the beast standing before him, but knew his life depended on it.

"And what do we have here?" the monster asked, almost sarcastically. "How old are you, boy?"

"I am eighteen, Sir," Peter lied.

"And what do you do?" he interrogated.

"I am an engineer, Sir," he lied again, but as politely as possible.

"Okay, you can get in that queue," he told the youngster, directing him to the left. He joined the queue in which the younger men seemed to be in the majority.

He remembered what William had told him only moments earlier, that if sent to the left he would survive tonight and wake in the morning, although he wasn't truly sure what he'd meant by it.

# CHAPTER 2
# TW0-NINE-EIGHT-SIX-ONE

"Everyone pick up your luggage and follow the guard. Schnell! Schnell! Quickly! Quickly!" the voice of the murderer was heard to boom.

When he'd been part of the roundup in Budapest, along with everyone else, Peter had been told to pack one small bag with a change of clothes and to bring all his valuables. Looking around now, it seemed like everyone else had also been given this same order and had followed it in detail. Now all the men in his line picked up their bags and suitcases and followed the guard ahead of them.

Both lines of people slowly walked toward the entrance of the sinister looking building, not knowing what waited for them inside the camp. As they reached the large stone arched entrance, they were greeted by a wonderful orchestra playing soothing classical music.

'How nice,' Peter thought.

This was the point where the two lines separated. Peter's line went straight ahead, whilst those in the right hand queue were directed to turn and go to the right. Peter hoped they didn't have too far to go, as the older people and young mothers looked exhausted, whilst the poor children looked extremely tired and ready for bed and a good night's sleep.

On and on they walked. It seemed the further they ventured inside the camp, the muddier the walk became. Peter was happy he'd worn his best shoes for the journey, although unhappy that they were now dirty and covered in filth.

"Halt!" the guard leading them shouted.

Peter looked around and he spotted a group of men dressed the same as William and Clause had been earlier, in striped pyjama looking uniforms and again all wearing Russian Army Trench coats.

"Everyone line up and remove your clothes," one of the men, whom Peter later learned was in the Sonderkommando, ordered. "Take off all your clothes and put them on top of your luggage so you know where to find them after your shower," the man barked again.

The line of men all did as ordered and now stood there naked and moving slowly towards a heavy metal door. Some were hiding their modesty by cupping their privates in their hands, but most didn't bother. There were now far more important things to worry about than modesty. Once inside the huge concrete walled room, Peter was surprised to hear a man close to him was quietly sobbing.

"What's the matter with you," he asked the man. "Why are you crying?"

"I have heard about this place," the man replied in tears. "I have heard this is how they kill us Jews. They seal us inside a big room and drop gas in through holes in the roof to exterminate everyone inside."

Upon hearing this, Peter took a good look around. Could this be true? He was now also terrified, and when he noticed scratch marks on the walls where victims must have tried to claw their way out, he felt even more so!

Suddenly the lights dimmed and some men began screaming, one man was even heard crying for his mother! A loud noise was then heard over the commotion. The noise turned into a loud gushing sound and then... cold water began spewing out of the shower heads above on the ceiling.

The instant relief was immense. Some men even began laughing hysterically, although not for long, as the freezing water landed on their naked bodies on this cold, early October evening in Poland began to take bite.

After only a couple of minutes, the water reduced to a trickle before stopping completely. Then the lights returned to bright again, so bright in fact that it hurt Peter's eyes and he blinked a few times to regain full vision. The huge doors were pulled open and the same voice was heard.

"Alle raus - Everyone out," the voice demanded.

Peter felt relieved to leave that room. Maybe it was what the stranger had told him which scared him so, but he wasn't sure. He just knew he wanted to be out.

"Find a uniform and get dressed quickly," the man from the Sonderkommando shouted, loud enough for everyone to hear.

'What does he mean – uniform?' Peter thought. He then noticed that the large pile of luggage and clothing had all disappeared.

"Excuse me," one man was heard to say politely, "Where are my clothes?" His question was answered by being hit on the backside by another Sonderkommando carrying a large wooden pole.

"Find a uniform and put it on!" the man barked at the poor man, who now looked shocked and was in real pain. "When you are in your uniform, all form a line and we will go to the administration block," the first Sonderkommando ordered.

Peter found a uniform more or less in his size, but when he looked for his shoes, they were gone. He almost asked as to their whereabouts but stopped himself, thinking better of it. He'd already realised that in this place, questions were to be answered and not asked.

Peter noticed a pile of wooden clog type shoes piled up in the corner of the room. These shoes were not even in pairs, but after searching for a few seconds, he managed t find a similar pair, although one was a little tight, while the other was a little loose. He made a mental note to mention it to William, if he was lucky enough to see him again.

After a few more minutes of slow walking, the men eventually reached another building, which Peter assumed was the administration block. They were told to form into two lines and enter the building, where they found two men sitting at a desk with large ledgers in front of each.

"What is your name?" they asked each man in turn, carefully writing each name in the left hand column of the page. When it was Peter's turn, he was asked the same question.

"What is your name?"

"Peter."

"Peter what?" the man said, looking at him with distain.

"Sorry Sir, it's Peter Florea," he replied.

After writing his name in the book, the man at the desk wrote something on a small piece of paper and gave it to him.

"Memorise this number and give this paper to the Tätowierer," the man ordered.

As he walked away, Peter took a quick glance at the paper he'd been given. Written upon it were five numbers – two-nine-eight-six-one – what did it mean, and why was he going to see a Tätowierer, whatever that was?

Walking through yet another door he saw four men dressed in the same uniform as he now wore, all sitting at separate desks with various pieces of equipment in front of them.

"Next," called one of the Tätowierers. Peter approached and stood before him. Without looking up, the man demanded, "Paper." Peter gave him the slip of paper with the number written on it. "Hold out your left arm and roll up the sleeve." Peter did as was ordered.

The man pulled a type of pen from his bag that had a very sharp needle attached. He grabbed Peter's arm, held it tight and began scratching something into the skin. It only took a few seconds but hurt like hell! After doing this, the man took out a rag soaked in black indelible ink and wiped it over the gouges.

"Next," the man shouted again, gesturing for Peter to move on.

Outside the men were all stood in a huddle, all looking at and comparing the numbers which had just been permanently etched upon their skin.

"My mother's going to kill me," Peter remarked. "She always made me promise never to get one of these."

One man looked up at him. "I don't think this will ever be a problem for you or your mother," he announced. Was he joking? What did he mean by this? Peter was confused.

After waiting for the rest of the men to receive their numerical tattoos and standing in the cold for almost an hour, finally a member of the Sonderkommando boomed out the command, "Follow me."

They walked down a muddy track with large wooden structures on either side. They were all painted black, which made them very difficult to see in the darkness of the night. What was not so hard to spot were the towers positioned every fifty yards or so, each containing men with machine guns pointing at them. Peter was very aware by now that one false move and his life would be over!

The Sonderkommando shouted for everyone to stop and to, "Listen very carefully." He then proceeded to shout out twenty numbers. He told the owners of these numbers, "You will sleep here. The man then pointed to one of the wooden structures and the twenty men disappeared inside. This act was repeated a few times, before the number of pyjama dressed men had dwindled. Finally, his number, Two-Nine-Eight-Six-One was called.

"Go in and find a place to sleep," he and his companions were ordered, and they all entered the wooden building numbered 'Hut 27.'

Once inside, although the light was dim, Peter was able to look around, however, the sights that greeted him were worse than grim! The large wooden hut, for that's what it was, a hut, he guessed was intended to house around thirty people, but doing a rough count he estimated there were at least seventy prisoners here.

He looked for a bed to sleep in but found there were none spare. In fact, it looked like there were at least three men to each bed, with no mattress provided. He later learned that in the past, they'd been given straw to make the beds more comfortable, but after time the straw became infested with bugs and maggots, making it better to sleep without.

"These men became so hungry that they actually began eating it," William Straus later informed him. Although Peter found this hard to believe, why would William lie to him?

As he was looking around and trying to decide where to sleep, a man approached. "Welcome to Hell!" the man said, offering his hand.

"Hello. My name is Peter," he replied.

"Names do not matter in this place," the man told him. "You are no longer human, you are now a dog. In fact, in this place you are treated worse than the dogs which barked at you and wanted to tear you apart when you arrived."

"But surely they will treat us better when we begin work?" Peter questioned.

"What do you mean?" the man asked, a little confused.

"I mean this is a work camp. We have been invited here to work," Peter said to this man, who by now had an astonished expression on his face. "After all, the camp motto is 'Arbeit Macht Frei' - 'Work Makes You Free.' This is one of the reasons why I volunteered."

The man almost choked when he heard this. "You volunteered! Are you stupid?" he demanded. "This is not a work camp!"

"No?" Peter queried.

"No!" the dirty faced man confirmed. "This is not a work camp, this is a death camp! They have not brought you here to work; they have brought you here to die!"

He dragged Peter back to the entrance of the hut. "You see those four chimneys with the black smoke spewing from them?" he asked, and Peter nodded in acknowledgement. "Those are the four crematoriums burning the bodies of those poor souls who have been gassed tonight. When you arrived on the cattle train tonight, you were placed into one of two lines. When you came into the camp, one of these lines went to the right. While you were lucky to go straight ahead, those poor bastards who went to the right are coming out of those chimneys now!"

"But they were old and frail, or young mothers with children," Peter gasped.

"Exactly," the man returned. "They are no use to the Nazis so the solution to the problem has been found – Death!"

"But they were only children," Peter said quietly. "They were only pure innocent children."

"My name is Franz," the man finally gave in and told him, before asking, "What on earth possibly made you volunteer to come to this Hell Hole?"

Peter went on to tell Franz how he'd heard the Germans were looking to send Jewish people to 'Work Camps,' and he thought that if he volunteered, then they would leave his parents alone.

"Are you stupid?" Franz asked again, stunned by what he'd just heard.

"Apparently so," Peter admitted, looking totally dejected. "How long have you been in here, Franz?" the youngster questioned.

"I have no idea," Franz replied with honesty. "Every day seems to last for a month, and every month is like a year. Nevertheless, I do know when I arrived here. It was in the spring of 1943, I remember it was April. What month is it now?"

"It's the seventeenth of October, 1943," Peter informed him.

"Shit! That means I have only been here for six months," Franz articulated. "It seems like at least two years since I walked into camp."

"Where do I sleep?" Peter questioned, looking around at the rows and rows of bunks piled three high, almost to the roof of the hut.

"You can sleep anywhere you like," Franz replied. "But take a tip from me and always sleep on the top bunk. The sicker these people get, the more difficult it is for them to get up to the top. Also, if you sleep below them, there is a good chance you will wake up covered in puke, or worse, shit! These poor men are rife with dysentery!"

"It smells so badly in here!" the young man claimed.

"Don't worry, Peter, if you are lucky and live long enough, you will get used to the stench."

Peter told Franz about the man who'd shot the baby's mother in the head and then threw the baby away. After giving him a brief description of the SS officer, he asked, "Who is that man?"

It sounds to me like you are talking about Heinz Kappler,"
Franz revealed. "He is a bastard, but he is nowhere near the
worst of the Nazis in this place."

"So who should I avoid?" Peter questioned.

"All of them, Peter," Franz almost laughed. "If you wish to
stay alive, you must never look them in the eyes. If they talk to
you, look at the floor. And if you ever see the Commandant of
the camp, Rudolph Höss, you must avoid him at all costs."

"Thank you for the advice," Peter said, appreciating the
chat with Franz, knowing there was no reason for him to talk to
the lad.

"No problem, Peter," the Polish man replied. "Now I
suggest you try to sleep. However, before then you must
memorise your number. If they ask who you are, NEVER use
your name, it no longer exists. And when they call your
number at roll call, if you do not answer immediately, it will be
very painful."

"Roll call? Peter queried.

"It happens every morning, and it's not a pleasant
experience. Try to sleep now. You will need all your strength
for tomorrow."

"What time is it lights out?" Pete questioned.

"Never," Franz informed the youngster. "The lights are
left on twenty-four hours a day, every day. Now get some
sleep."

Peter found a small space on one of the top bunks and
even though he thought that he wouldn't, being so exhausted,
he soon fell into a deep sleep, where he hoped he'd dream of
better and happier times.

# CHAPTER 3
# NEW LIFE BEGINS

His first full day in Auschwitz began when a shrill whistle woke everyone at four in the morning, although he didn't know it was four in the morning as there were no clocks anywhere. Anyway, what did time matter when you were in this hellhole of a place?

The Sonderkommando blowing the whistle interrupted a beautiful dream where he was walking in the park with his mother and father. He was carrying a large wicker picnic basket full of cold meats and freshly baked bread, the smell of which was assaulting his nostrils in a wonderful way. In the few seconds between sleeping and waking, he wondered if being in the camp had all been a nightmare. The reality of the situation soon hit home as the chaos began.

"Come on, Peter, get up," Franz instructed as he approached. "It would not be good to be late."

"What happens now?" Peter enquired with a feeling of unease.

"Follow me," Franz instructed.

Peter went with his new friend and everyone else to the wash room, where several large bowls of freezing cold water were waiting for the prisoners to clean themselves as best as possible.

Peter saw two rows of ten toilet seats staggered opposite each other, enough for the twenty men who were already seated there pissing and taking a shit whilst seated in front of the thirty or so men waiting to do the same. Peter was horrified to see this, but realising there was no room for modesty in this place, when it was his turn, he just got on with it.

They were not really toilet seats, just two long planks of wood with ten holes in each and positioned above a trough where the excrement fell. This would be emptied twice a week by one or more unlucky prisoners ordered to do the job. Peter hoped with all his heart that he would not be selected for this!

After washing and taking his morning ablutions, he followed Franz back to Hut 27, where he found a man standing by the side of a large bowl of something hot and steamy, holding a ladle. As the man scooped out some of the liquid and put it into a large tin mug, Peter looked at the muddy brown fluid suspiciously, and then at Franz.

"What the hell is this?" he queried.

"It's supposed to be coffee," was the reply. "Drink it, Peter, it's all you'll get for a few more hours."

It tasted as disgusting as it looked. However, following the advice of his new friend, the youngster forced himself to finish it.

"Alle raus! Everyone out for roll call," the member of the Sonderkommando demanded, blowing his whistle again as though his life depended on it, although, Peter thought, maybe it did.

All the prisoners were ordered to line up in rows of ten and to spread out one yard apart, one hundred men to each group. They stood there for fifteen minutes before a large open top car arrived. Peter shuddered with fear when he heard the name of the man inside. It was Rudolph Höss, the camp commandant.

The car door was opened for him and he stepped out, cane in hand, and walked up and down among the men standing before him. He studied each one of them, looking at their faces and staring them in the eye with a gaze of steal. Peter could see that he was a truly fearsome character.

Every now and then, Höss touched one of the men on the shoulder and they were instantly dragged away by the

Sonderkommando. Peter wondered what would happen to them, what would be their fate? Maybe they'd been selected for that day's work party, although the ferocity of the way they'd been dragged away made him think otherwise and he feared for their safety.

The member of the Sonderkommando who'd blown the whistle earlier was sent back inside the now empty hut. He emerged a few moments later with a scrap of paper in his hand, which he gave to the officer in charge. Peter dared to glance at Franz, who in turn nodded to confirm the identity of the officer. It was Heinz Kappler.

The paper carried by the Sonderkommando contained the numbers of those poor souls who had perished during the night. There were nine men who'd gone to sleep that night, but had not woken this morning. In a weird way, Peter felt a little jealous of these men, as for them, this nightmare was now over.

"Franz, without looking in his direction, whispered to Peter, "With nine dead, maybe we can find you a blanket for tonight."

The young man did not like the callous nature of what he'd said or the way he'd said it, but he thought that having a blanket would certainly be a distinct advantage. Last night, he was bloody cold!

Rudolph Höss got back into his car and was driven away. Peter thought he was maybe being taken to the next gathering of prisoners to select more poor men for whatever he had planned for them.

Under the watchful eye of SS officer Heinz Kappler the roll call began, and would go on for more than one hour. This caused many of the weaker among them to struggle to remain standing. Those who sank to their knees would be punished by the stock of a rifle being rammed into their face or stomach, whichever was easier to access.

"Three-One-seven-eight-Nine," a Sonderkommando called.

"Here," a weak voice was heard to confirm. This process was repeated over and over again, until finally Peter's number was called.

"Two-Nine-Eight-Six-One," he heard.

"Here," he replied, relieved to have been vigilant enough to have heard his number being called, and even happier to have remembered it.

"Everyone who arrived last night, you must report now to the administration block to be assigned your work detail," Heinz Kappler announced. Once again, fear coursed through Peter's veins.

"You will be okay, Peter," Franz offered. "If you were to be murdered, it would have been done by now and you would be burning in the crematorium." The words were bleak, but the sentiment was bizarrely comforting.

Daylight was just breaking through as he reached the administration block. He was forced to line up again and wait his turn to be seen and assigned his work detail. As he waited, he noticed a familiar figure walking past. He almost called out his name but remembered what William and Franz had told him. "Do not use names in here, only numbers."

Not knowing William's number, he waved to him and hoped he would recognise him from last night when they'd met in the cattle truck. That really did seem so long ago now, was it really only less than ten hours since that meeting?

"Hello my friend," William said when reaching him. "How are you?"

"I'm okay," Peter replied, "but I am very cold." As he said this, he looked at William's Russian Army coat. "When will I be given my coat?" William almost choked as Peter asked this.

"I'm very sorry, Peter," he said quietly so no one could hear him call him by his name. "Only members of the Sonderkommando and others doing what he SS consider as essential work are given coats to keep warm."

"But if it gets any colder, I'm going to freeze to death!" Peter pleaded.

"Look my friend," William said quietly, "whatever work they assign you, please try to stick it out for as long as you can. In the meantime, I will attempt to get you transferred so you can work with Claus and me."

"Thank you," Peter said, without knowing the real work that William and his co-worker performed. Nevertheless, whatever it was, it had to be better than what he was about to receive.

William's parting words to the youngster were, "Peter, until we can get you assigned to work with us, just try to stay alive."

"Number?" the man sitting at the desk demanded as Peter stood before him.

"Two-Nine-Eight-Six-One," Peter confirmed.

The desked man looked up at the young lad standing before him, sure that he couldn't handle the work and would soon be dead; a wry smile came upon his face.

"You will join the work detail at the stone quarry," he informed Peter.

"Thank you, Sir," Peter replied defiantly. If they thought they'd broken him, he wasn't going to show it and give these Nazis the satisfaction!

Outside the admin block, a group of men were forming. A guard quickly joined them and they were soon on their way.

Peter could not believe how far away the quarry was. They'd been walking for what seemed to him like an hour but could have been less as time went so slowly in this evil place, making it hard to judge. What he did know for certain, was that some of the men already looked dead on their feet. They were so thin, almost like human skeletons! He was convinced that some of them would not make it to the quarry, let alone still be alive at the end of the working day! They finally walked through an entrance. They'd arrived.

The sight before him made his heart sink. It was a huge area about the size of two football pitches, with huge rocks being broken by men with pickaxes into smaller rocks that the prisoners would then carry by hand, around fifty or more yards to deposit into a pile.

Peter later discovered that the men with the pickaxes were actually paid civilians from the local towns and villages. They would work a seven hour day, three hours followed by a one hour break and then back to work for another three hours. For this they were paid, and handsomely.

Peter guessed the Nazis could not trust the campmates with the pickaxes in case they used them to attack the guards, even though these guards were heavily armed with rifles and pistols. In fact, all the time that Peter toiled in the quarry, he always felt the existence of a rifle being pointed at him.

The civilians worked in shifts, whilst Peter and his workmates were forced to work eleven hours or more, with just enough of a break to eat dinner.

Dinner – This was a word laughably used to describe the meagre offerings given to the prisoners during a twenty minute break.

Every day it was the same, a type of soup made from the left over peelings from vegetables used to feed the SS officers and guards, as well as some of the lucky Sonderkommando.

It always had an awful smell, as though the vegetable peelings were already rotten before being used to make the soup. However, by the time they'd been told to break for lunch, the men were so ravenous they would have eaten a dead dog. Mind you, a dead dog would probably have been more nutritious. If you were very lucky, you just might find a small piece of potato or carrot floating within your portion.

When it was his turn, the guard poured around half a litre of the 'so called' soup into a large tin mug and presented it to Peter, along with a small piece of stale bread. The first mouthful of the foul smelling liquid almost made him wretch, but he forced it down, as he must keep his strength up to give himself the best chance of survival.

"Back to work!" the guard ordered.

You could almost hear the audible groan as the men forced their weary bodies back to the mundane, soul destroying task of carrying rocks from one side of the quarry to the other, a job which could have been made much easier by supplying wheel barrows. However, this would not have been so much fun for these vile monsters, who obviously received great joy out of watching these poor men suffer.

Finally, the guard blew the whistle to signify the end of the day. At the final count, four men were dead, with four more men ordered to carry the bodies back to the camp. Peter pitied these men, as he thought there was a good chance that at least one of them would also die because of this.

An hour later, they arrived back at Auschwitz Birkenau, which he discovered was the actual name of the camp where he now resided.

Peter hadn't realised there were actually two camps here. The smaller camp, 'Auschwitz One,' was situated about one mile away. This is where the sign was that Peter had seen in the propaganda he'd read, the sign that had caused his confusion and made him want to volunteer to come here, the sign that read "Work Makes You Free." What it should really say is, "Work in This Place Will Kill You For Sure!"

The young lad couldn't believe it when he finally arrived back exhausted at Hut 27. All he wanted to do was collapse on his bunk, but no, yet another roll call was called.

Peter supposed it was to discover how many of the men, who'd begun the day had actually made it to the end. The number of men from Hut 27 who had indeed died that day was incredible – fifteen. Still, many more poor souls would have died that day in the gas chamber!

He looked to the chimneys and could see the black, putrid smoke still gushing from their tops. He could see the pieces of ash floating through the air and thought it looked like black snow!

# CHAPTER 4
# THE ANGEL OF DEATH

Peter was taking a well deserved rest and dozing on his 'bed' after the evening's roll call when his friend interrupted his slumber.

Come, Peter," Franz said as he approached. "Come and meet my friends."

"Meet your friends?" Peter questioned, whilst attempting to shake off his drowsiness.

"Yes," Franz confirmed. "I have friends in other huts dotted around this camp."

"Can we visit them safely," a concerned Peter questioned.

"Yes, my friend," Franz replied almost smiling. "We are allowed to visit other huts, or just get some exercise for an hour or so after roll call is finished. When this free time is over, they sound a siren that signals we have fifteen minutes to return to our own hut. After this, they will sound a second siren, signalling curfew time has ended. If you are caught outside after this, the guards in the towers will use you for target practise, so make sure this never happens."

They walked for a few minutes before Franz led Peter into Hut 44. He was amazed to see the difference between the people housed here to that of his own dwelling. Not only were there men present, but also women and children.

"Who are these people?" Peter questioned.

"They are my friends," Franz replied. "They are gypsies from Germany."

"From Germany?" a confused Peter asked, looking for confirmation.

"Yes, Peter, these animals even imprison their own kind!" Franz stated.

The youngster found this information totally amazing. How a nation could be at war with people from its own country was unbelievable to Peter, but then the same could also be said about the German Jews languishing here in this filth. The fact was that some of the Jewish men locked up in Auschwitz actually fought in the German army during the Great War, less than twenty-five years ago.

"Peter, this is my friend Oswald," he said, introducing the youngster to a much older man, or at least he looked much older.

"Pleased to meet you," Peter smiled, shaking the other man's hand.

"Likewise," Oswald replied.

Oswald looked to be in his fifty's, but was actually only forty-two years of age. Time spent in Auschwitz had aged him greatly, although he still possessed rugged good looks and piercing blue eyes, along with long black shoulder length hair and a matching beard. Peter imagined that when he was clean and well dressed, he would have been a fine figure of a man amd very good looking.

"How long have you been here?" Oswald questioned the young lad.

"I arrived last night," Peter remarked, although still not believing that he'd only arrived less than twenty-four hours ago. "How about you and your people, when did you come here?"

"We were rounded up in Bavaria in 1942 and taken from camp to camp," Oswald instructed. "We eventually arrived at Auschwitz Birkenau in March of this year, nineteen forty-three. At least I presume it's still the same year, is it still nineteen forty-three?" he joked.

Peter made the observation to Franz, that Oswald and the people in this structure looked considerably healthier to those in their own hut.

"They are treated better because, as they are not from the Jewish community, they are not considered to be a real enemy. They also receive more food because of the work they do. Most of the men in here are builders. They are responsible for maintaining the structures of the camp."

"Maintaining structures, like keeping the crematoriums running?" Peter queried.

"Well yes," Franz confirmed, but then stated. "But Peter, someone has to do it."

"Wait," Peter demanded angrily, reverting to something said previously. "You say Jewish people are the enemy to Germany?"

"No," Franz interrupted. "Not Germany, the Nazis in charge of the country. I honestly believe that most German people, including those soldiers at the front line, don't even know about these camps."

"But why do they consider me as their enemy?" Peter asked incredulously. "I've never done anything to hurt anyone in my life!"

"You were unlucky to have been born into a family practising the Jewish faith at a time when a silly little man with a stupid moustache declared his hatred of you all, and persuaded thousands, if not millions to join the Nazi party and do the same."

"It's all so unfair," was all that Peter could quietly offer.

"Oswald, what's happened to that man?" Franz questioned his friend, whilst pointing to a man sitting on the edge of a bunk with a soiled bandage wrapped around his eyes.

"That monster, Josef Mengele," Oswald stressed. "That's what happened to that poor bastard. His name is Lemmie."

"What happened?" Peter questioned.

"When Lemmie was working at the construction site, the men received a visit from the camp doctor, Josef Mengele, known to everyone in Auschwitz as, 'Todesengel' - 'The Angel of Death.

He made all the men line up so he could examine them. He then studied them closely, particularly looking into their eyes. When he came to Lemmie, he thought he'd struck gold as Lemmie had green eyes.

Tapping him on the shoulder, he was taken away forcibly to the hospital block, Block Ten at Auschwitz One, where Josef Mengele carries out his experiments."

"Experiments," Peter butted in. "What do you mean, experiments?"

"Just listen to this, Peter," Franz instructed the lad, and Oswald continued with his story.

"For the next two weeks, poor Lemmie was receiving daily injections in his right eye with no anaesthetic. Mengele was injecting colouring dye into his eye to see if he could change the colour from green to blue. After two weeks, he gave up on the right eye and started on the left, using a different composition of dye."

"Did it work?" asked Peter innocently, blissfully unaware of the callous nature of his question.

"At the moment he's still blind in both eyes, but we're hoping he might get a little vision back soon. We certainly hope so, because if not, we have no idea of what would be his fate."

"What do you mean?" questioned a naive Peter.

"I mean that if he stays blind he will be no use to the SS, so there is a good chance he will be sent to the gas chamber and then the crematorium."

"Shit!" was all Peter could say, the seriousness of the situation he was in now becoming clearer. "What does he look like, this Mengele?" He asked this so he could recognise the monster, and then steer clear of him.

"Josef Mengele dresses in a white doctor's coat and always has a stethoscope around his neck. He is the man you would have seen when you arrived last night," Oswald told the young man. "He is the man at the cattle truck ramp who decides who lives and who dies in this place."

"But I thought that was Heinz Kappler?" Peter queried.

"No," Oswald smirked. "Heinz Kappler makes the decision as to who should go left or right, but Josef Mengele decides which of those in the right line should be spared, usually for his experiments and normally with young twins. Believe me, Peter, compared to Mengele, Heinz Kappler is a saint!"

Suddenly the siren sounded. "Quickly Peter," Franz ordered. "We have to go."

"Quick, take this," Oswald said to his friend, putting a piece of bread into the hands of both. "Come back tomorrow and we will have more food for you. Now go, do not get caught after the curfew. You must live to fight another day."

The three men shook hands and Peter and Franz left Hut 44. They quickly made their way back, arriving just a minute or two before the second of the second siren pierced the air. They were safe, at least for another night.

After another cup of revolting coffee, it was time to sleep, if that was at all possible. Tomorrow would bring another day. However, what would the next day bring? The answer to this question was - nothing much different.

Peter would find that every day in Auschwitz Birkenau was the same as the last. The only difference was the total number of deaths that occurred on a daily basis.

After a couple of weeks in camp, Peter was almost immune to death and thought nothing of it. He did feel great sadness for those who'd passed away in their sleep, but considered it as a far better alternative to being sent to the gas chamber, or being worked to death at the stone quarry.

All the time he was working at the quarry, his mind was taking him to other places. He would daydream about his younger days at school in Budapest, playing football in the playground during the lunch break or having a game of kiss chase with the girls. He remembered the day when this all changed for him, the day he'd had the Star of David emblazoned on his clothes. All the boys and girls whom he'd considered as his best friends all turned against him. He was now treated like scum!

One thing he always looked forward to in the camp was his daily evening visit to Hut 44, and meeting up with Oswald and the gypsies. Peter always felt welcome with these people, and had made a few friends.

He'd also been told a few more horror stories about Josef Mengele, the Angel of Death. The worst one he'd been told of was about a pair of three year old twin sisters. They'd been chosen for an extremely vile experiment, where Mengele had amputated the left leg on one and the right leg on the other.

They then had their wounds stitched together and were allowed to spend three months convalescing in the hospital wing. After this, the 'Angel of Death' attempted to make them walk as one. When he discovered this to be impossible, Mengele had them euthanized.

Another favourite of Mengele's was to take older men and women and make them stand in freezing cold water for hours until near death. At the instant it was believed they had died from hyperthermia, Mengele would have them removed from the water and attempted to revive them. Those who survived would have the process repeated the next day, and the next, on and on until eventually they perished.

Peter observed that those who died on the first day were the lucky ones!

"Josef Mengele, what a bastard!" he cried.

# CHAPTER 5
# NEW DAY – NEW JOB

Peter had now been in Auschwitz for four weeks. The one day he always looked forward to was Sunday. He recollected how at the end of his first week he'd woken one morning to almost daylight. Worried that he'd missed the roll call, so was in serious trouble, he woke Franz in a very fraught state of panic!

"Franz, wake up," he'd demanded. "Where is everyone? Have the guards all deserted the camp?"

Franz began to laugh. "No Peter, they haven't abandoned us. It's Sunday. Even us prisoners get a day off, although I rather think it's for the benefit of the guards and not us," he said and laughed again.

"So what do we do today," questioned young Peter.

"Whatever you want," replied Franz. "You can go wherever you want and see whoever you want, but only until the siren blasts tonight. Go for a walk, Peter. Get to know the place, but be back here before the second siren sounds."

Peter thought this was a good idea. He even thought it might be a good opportunity to find the whereabouts of William and Claus. He discovered there would be no new arrivals on a Sunday; so the two of them would also have a day of freedom.

After his usual morning mug of 'slop,' as he called it, he went off for his big adventure. This place was huge, much bigger than he could ever have imagined.

Auschwitz Birkenau felt different today, not so dangerous. He even thought there were less guards walking around the camp on foot, although of course the men in the towers still

41

had their machine guns trained and ready to fire at a split seconds notice.

One thing he observed which made him feel extra happy about was that, being at the end of the week, there was no Heinz Kappler, Joseph Mengele, and definitely no Rudolph Höss in attendance. He imagined them all curled up with their wives and loved ones listening to the radio and having fun. Although the thought of Heinz Kappler having fun, or having loved ones for that matter, was a thought too difficult for Peter to imagine!

Four weeks later, he'd gotten into a Sunday routine. He always started the day with a visit to Oswald and the Hut 44 family. Although it might sound selfish, they always had more food there for breakfast and didn't mind sharing with him.

He enjoyed playing with the gypsy children. They'd invented a chasing game played with one shoe. A child would grab hold of a shoe and throw it as far as they could, then all the children; about ten of them, would chase the shoe as though life depended on it. The first one to reach the shoe would pick it up, wave it in the air, and then throw it as far as they could, beginning the process all over again.

After watching the children playing for a couple of hours, Peter was sure there were no winners of this game. However, the kids all loved it and that's all that mattered.

During his second Sunday, the youngster had discovered that the camp orchestra, who had played beautiful classical music the night he'd arrived, actually gave a concert every Sunday afternoon in the main square.

Peter loved going to this concert and listening to them play their beautiful music, even if it was in the place where they hanged the prisoners who tried to escape. In fact, as the orchestra played, they were in the shadow of the gallows.

Another good thing about attending this concert on the first occasion was that he found William in the audience. Luckily, he hadn't forgotten Peter and told him he was still waiting for an opening to become vacant for the lad. He told him to stay alive just a little bit longer. This gave Peter the impetus to keep going.

When toiling in the stone quarry, the thought that every day could be his last day working there kept him going. Finally, that day came during his fourth Sunday morning.

He was relaxing on his bunk, slops in hand, when he heard a familiar voice greet him.

"Good morning, my friend Peter," William grinned. "How are you, this fine morning?"

"I was feeling okay a few moments ago," Peter admitted, "but I feel even better now for seeing you."

"I have news for you," William announced.

"Good I hope?" Peter queried.

"I think so," William revealed. "You can begin working with me and Claus tomorrow. Apparently they are gearing up to bring even more poor souls here, so need more of us to help with the clear up."

Peter didn't much like the sound of this, but whatever the reason, it would be better than the work he had now, where in the quarry, more and more men died daily from exhaustion. He knew that if he stayed there, he could soon be one of them.

"What happens now?" the youngster questioned.

"Tomorrow, after roll call you must meet me at the administration block. If any guard stops you on the way and asks why you are not going to work, just show them your number. You have been registered for work with us."

"What about the men in the towers?" Peter asked suspiciously. "Has anyone told them?"

"As long as you don't run or make a bolt for the fence or attack a guard, you will be fine," William laughed. "See you in the morning."

"See you at the concert this afternoon?" Peter asked his friend.

"Maybe," William answered, making his way to the door.

The air smelled sweeter and there was a renewed spring in his step, as he went with William and Claus to begin his new work with them. Even though he had no idea of what the work really entailed, at least it would be better than working at the stone quarry. At the very least, he thought there was a better chance of his ending the day still alive, especially after being gifted his new coat.

He felt warm for the first time in weeks. Yes, Peter felt like a weight had been lifted from his young shoulders, but then he realised where they were walking to, the arrival of the transportation cattle truck carrying fresh blood to the camp.

'Those poor people,' Peter thought. 'They don't have any idea of what lies ahead for them.'

"Now Peter, stay close and do not get in the way of the guards," William instructed. "Hold back for now. Our work begins when the SS have cleared the train and the area."

The scene reminded him of his own arrival a few weeks back. The crescendo of noise echoing through the air and the mass hysteria of the dogs barking, whilst the SS officers shouted their orders, brought it all home to him. He noticed the looks on the faces of the arrivals as they alighted from the cattle wagon, noting it was a mixture of confusion and pure fear, but mostly fear!

He watched as the arrivals were separated into two lines. It broke his heart when he saw the innocent children clinging to their mothers' hands, whilst also still holding their teddy bears and dollies close to their chests to give them comfort.

It made his blood boil when he thought of these children. They had waited millions of years to be born, but then after living only a very small percentage of the life they should have been entitled to, it was to be ended by a mad lunatic with a flick of the wrist! What gave this man, or any man, the right to decide who should live and who should die?

"Keep calm, Peter," William instructed, sensing the youngster was becoming a little too emotional.

"Sorry," Peter offered. "But it's so unfair!"

"You're correct my friend," Claus said joining the conversation. "But unless you want to join them and go to the gas chamber today and maybe take us with you, you have to control your feelings."

"Sorry," Peter repeated.

Claus gave him a reassuring pat on the back as the three continued to survey the scene. All around them now was just pure chaos. When he saw the women and children join the queue to go to the right, Peter had to try with all his strength not to shout out, 'Don't go there. They are sending you to your death!' However, he knew what the result would be, should he do so.

As the masses began to dwindle, he caught his first sight of the man in the white coat. He was on bended knee studying the children and deciding their fate.

"Is that?" Peter began.

"Mengele," William interrupted. "Yes, that is Josef Mengele, the Angel of Death."

"Bastard!" was all Peter could comment.

He briefly looked at the man whom everyone feared, and feared with good reason. What Peter couldn't believe was how normal he looked. He wondered how tough he would be in a street fight, with no armed guards to protect him. He surmised that Doctor Josef Mengele was a typical bully, abusing his position of power and loving it!

It made him feel physically sick when he watched Mengele waving to the right or left, deciding which child should live and who should die. He also knew that the children who survived today would probably not be alive for much longer, and their treatment would not be a painless one.

"Come on Peter," William said. "Let's get to work."

Stepping inside the cattle truck rekindled dreadful memories of his own transportation. However, what he didn't remember about that journey was the awful smell that assaulted his nostrils as he stepped aboard.

"This must be what death smells like," he whispered to William.

"Trust me," William replied, "you will never get used to it."

"I don't think I want to," Peter confessed.

They dragged out the bodies of the lost souls who never made it. There were only five dead this time, making the young man think it must have been a much shorter journey than the one he'd embarked upon. After laying the bodies in the trolley, the three went back to collect their luggage and then gave the floor a quick swill with a bucket of water, before moving to the next carriage.

Not only was this work backbreaking, it was also heartbreaking. To ease his pain, Peter constantly kept telling himself that it had to be better than carrying rocks around all day.

What Peter had not realised was that the three of them were only one of five teams doing this work. With each team emptying three carriages, the train was soon empty and ready to return to wherever it had to be, in order to collect even more 'lambs' to bring to the slaughter!

Whilst the dead were wheeled away for their appointment with the ovens, Peter, William and Claus were tasked with first taking the deceased's luggage to the storage facility, situated close to the administration block inside Auschwitz Birkenau. He was thankful that his job did not entail removing the clothes from the dead. This was a job carried out by the Sonderkommando, prior to the body being turned to ash.

After they'd completed the task they walked swiftly to the shower block, where they saw the 'survivors' were all standing naked outside waiting to take a shower. All the men in the queue looked petrified and Peter wanted to reassure them by shouting, 'You're all going to be fine. It really is only water,' but he had to stop himself from getting involved.

Again, all these people had been ordered in advance to pile their clothes on top of their cases, and to remember where they'd left them for when they came out of the shower room. As soon as the last of them was inside and the heavy steel doors were slammed shut, Peter and his colleagues were hard at work again. They had ten to fifteen minutes to totally remove all the clothing and cases containing these peoples' valuables and get them back to the storage facility.

After this work was completed, it was repeated again, but this time at the gas chambers. This time it was more leisurely work, as sadly nobody would be re-emerging to look for and claim their belongings.

This time, when inside the storage facility, Peter was able to take a better look at his new surroundings. He couldn't believe the size of this place. There were suitcases piled floor to ceiling as far as the eye could see. However, when he saw the towers of children's' shoes, dollies and cuddly toys, he became very emotional. How he hated these murdering bastards!

"That's it, Peter," William informed the youngster. "Work is over for your first night, but the hard work begins in the morning."

He gave instructions to the lad to get some sleep, also telling him he was no longer required to attend roll call and was now allowed to sleep in a little later than the rest of the men in this hut.

William also told him that as soon as one became available, Peter would take a bunk in the much nicer dwelling where the people who did this work all lived together.

"How will I know when work begins in the morning?" Peter questioned, not wishing to be late.

"We will come for you," William instructed. "Sleep well, my friend. And don't have too many nightmares."

# CHAPTER 6
# KANADA

Although he had no reason to wake, the sound of the morning whistle resonating around the walls woke not only the rest of Hut 27, but also Peter. He lay there as he watched the rest of the inmates going about their business, preparing themselves for morning roll call. Even though he didn't feel entitled to it, he did get up and helped himself to a cup of the morning 'slops,' before returning to his bunk. He was just about to doze off again when the man from the Sonderkommando approached.

"What are you doing here?" the man demanded. "Why are you not out there with the rest of the prisoners attending the roll call?"

The Sonderkommando was just about to hit Peter on the bottom of his feet with his thick stick, when the youngster shouted at him.

"Stop, I no longer work at the stone quarry." He then went on to tell the man standing before him about the new work he had with William and Claus.

"Oh congratulations," the Sonderkommando laughed. "You have joined the Aufräumungskommando working at the Effektenlager. Good for you."

Peter had no idea what this man was talking about, as he'd never heard of the place he spoke of or the organisation he supposedly now belonged to. He made a mental note to ask William about it later in the day.

"Just you behave yourself and do not get caught stealing," the Sonderkommando said quietly, whilst coming close to his face. "Only the SS and the Nazis are allowed to be stealing from us Jews." As he said this, he spat on the floor. This confused Peter, as he always thought that members of the Sonderkommando were on the side of his captors.

"Well Peter, I hope we meet again soon," Franz said with his hand held out, waiting to be shaken. This made the lad wonder what his friend was talking about.

"What do you mean," a confused Peter questioned. "Of course we'll meet again, later, when I return from work."

"Somehow I don't think so," Franz observed. "Whatever happens, it's been good knowing you, Peter. God bless and take care of you always."

As he watched his friend leave the building, he wondered what was going on. First, the Sonderkommando made his comments and now Franz. It made him wonder if he was doing the right thing by taking this work. He would soon find out.

"Come on, Peter," he heard a voice say. It was William, who'd come to collect him as promised.

"I must have dozed off aain," Peter admitted. "What time is it?"

"It's time for work," William informed him, almost laughing at his state of drowsiness. He then said something that surprised the youngster. "Get all your things together and let's go."

"My things," Peter queried. "Why do I need my things, and what things do I need? I don't have any things! The Germans took all my 'things' the night I arrived!"

"Okay, but get ready because you're moving today." William instructed.

"Where to?" they youngster queried.

"You are moving in with us at the Effektenlager," William revealed. This was the second time Pete had heard this place mentioned this morning.

"But I like it here," he stated.

"You cannot stay here," William said sternly. "Trust me, Peter, you do NOT want to stay here."

"Why?" Peter demanded.

"You don't want to know."

"I do!"

"Okay, I'll tell you, but there's nothing you can do about it," William told the youngster.

Peter now had a strange, butterfly feeling in the pit of his stomach. He half expected to be informed of the reason for the urgency of his leaving today, but was still shocked and saddened when he heard the words coming from William's mouth.

"You cannot stay here because the occupants of Hut 27 are booked for the gas chamber tonight."

"When, what time?" a sad Peter questioned.

"It doesn't matter, Peter," William replied.

"What time?" an insistent Peter demanded.

"As soon as they arrive back from the work party," William stated.

"Bastards," Peter exclaimed. "They'll get one more day of work out of them before killing them! The murdering bastards!" he repeated angrily.

William had an idea of what his young workmate was thinking and wanted to nip it in the bud.

"You cannot help your friend and you cannot warn your friend," he ordered the lad. "If you do, you would burn with him in the crematorium tonight."

"At least death would be quick, instead of rotting inside this place for months on end," Peter remarked.

"Peter, you have to snap out of this melancholy, or you will never survive Auschwitz Birkenau," William advised.

"William, am I now the enemy?" Peter asked seriously, making the observation.

"Of course you're not!" William replied. Although he was trying to reassure him, he was getting angry now. "Now come on," he demanded. "Get your shit together and let's make a move." Peter did as was told.

After taking a final look around Hut 27 he followed William to his new place of work, albeit reluctantly. He was surprised to find himself back at the storage facility where they'd been the previous evening.

"Is this the place they call Effektenlager?" Peter asked his friend.

"That is the official name, Peter, but everyone calls it by its slang name of Kanada," his friend and work colleague instructed.

"Why?"

"That is a good question," William remarked, and then went on to tell him the reason.

"Well it all began with the girls who work here. All day long, they daydream about the camp being liberated, and a big strong man falling in love with them and taking them to a new life in Kanada. They also say that because of the work they do here, this building seems like the land of plenty, hence all through the camp, it's known as Kanada. Even the SS officers and Gestapo refer to it as Kanada."

"It's also far easier to pronounce," Peter laughed.

"Oh Peter, you make a joke," William laughed, slapping him on the back.

"Wait," Peter demanded. "You said the girls who work here. You mean there are girls in this camp, still alive?"

"Of course my friend, there are many girls here in Auschwitz Birkenau," William instructed. "In fact nearly all the prisoners who now work in Kanada are female. Even the guards here are mostly women."

"But they are worse than the male guards, believe me," Claus piped in.

"He's correct," William confirmed. "Most of the female SS officers stationed in Kanada are bitches! However, one or two of them can be quite pleasant towards us in the Kanada kommando."

"Wait, what, the Kanada Kommando?" Peter questioned.

"We are officially known as the Aufräumungskommando, but Kanada Kommando is the slang term for the cleanup squad," William explained. "We are known as the cleanup squad of Kanada."

As the three of them were speaking with each other, a familiar figure loomed close. They all looked at the floor when they realised whom the frame belonged to – It was Heinz Kappler.

"You must be the new Jew," Kappler announced, looking at Peter with total distain. He put his stick under the young lad's chin, lifting his face as he continued. "Work hard and we will get along just fine. However, Jew Boy, if you are ever caught stealing, I will have you sent to Doctor Mengele and have him remove your bollocks and have them displayed in the main square. Do we understand each other?"

"Yes sir," Peter mumbled.

"DO YOU UNDERSTAND?" Kappler shouted, demanding an answer.

"YES SIR," Peter shouted, hoping his raised voice would not get him in trouble on his first day here.

"That's better Jew Boy," Kappler commented. "When I ask you a question I expect an answer which I can hear."

Having made his case, Kappler walked away and the three men could begin breathing again.

"So I am now a member of the Kanada Kommando," Peter stated. "I am no better than the Sonderkommando."

"What do you mean by that?" Claus asked the lad.

"I mean the Sonderkommando are bullies," the youngster began. "They must enjoy inflicting misery on these poor, innocent people, otherwise why would they volunteer to assist the SS?"

"Volunteer!" William replied angrily, incensed by this stupidity. "They did not volunteer for the work; they were selected by the Gestapo on pain of death. They are carrying out orders of Rudolph Höss personally. In fact, to be honest, they have been ordered to do this work by Hitler himself!

When you see them herding the arrivals into the gas chamber, especially the women and children, do you think they enjoy this? No Peter, of course not.

Peter, you, Claus and I see death every day, but not on the scale of the Sonderkommando. Do you know that after these hundreds of people have met their deaths, it's these men who have to go inside the gas chamber and bring the naked bodies outside and move them all to the crematorium? It is then their job to shovel the bodies into the ovens and watch the poor bastards' burn and be turned to ash, the same ash that constantly floats through the Auschwitz air!"

"Sorry," Peter offered his friend. "I didn't know."

"But do you know the worst thing about being Sonderkommando, my friend?" William continued.

"No."

"Then I will tell you. The worst thing about being in the Sonderkommando is that when they go into the gas chamber to collect the bodies, they never know when the day will come when the heavy metal doors will be slammed closed behind them and locking them inside with the corpses. The 'Cyclone

B' would drop through the hatch in the roof, and they themselves will end up in the ovens!

No my friend, not one of these men volunteered to be in the Sonderkommando, and don't you forget it!"

"Calm down William," Claus pleaded. "Peter didn't know any of this before, but he does now."

"I'm sorry, William," Peter offered, feeling a little sad and ashamed to have upset his friend.

"That's okay," said William, calming down a little now. "I get angry because I've had friends in the Sonderkommando who have had this happen to them."

"What did Kappler mean about me stealing?" Peter questioned.

William went on to explain to Peter that the work he was now about to begin in Kanada was considered to be the best work available in the camp. He would now have plenty of opportunity to procure certain items and build up a nice little nest egg for when this situation ended; items like jewellery, especially diamonds, which the prisoners had brought with them to buy food and pay for their keep. Obviously this would never have happened, but the Germans thought these items were now their property, and anyone caught stealing from them would be severely punished.

"They often do a search in the sorting room, Peter," William informed the lad. "If you ever have anything on you, pop it in your mouth. If they wish to search you personally, you can swallow it and shit it out later."

"Do you have anything stashed away for a rainy day?" Peter asked his friend.

He answered with a smile and then said, "I'm saying nothing, but if you're careful, Peter, when this is over, you could be quite well off."

"But what would happen if we get caught with the merchandise?" the youngster questioned.

"Then, as Kappler said, you would be Doctor Josef Mengele's plaything. Even worse, you could be sent for interrogation by the Gestapo and they would torture you until you gave them the names of all the people you know who are thieving from them, and then they would kill you! For this reason, do not tell anyone else what you're doing, so they cannot give you away to the authorities, and this includes me!" William stressed.

"But you told me that you're doing it," Peter observed. "You told me with a smile."

"Shit!" was William's reaction. "I hope I can trust you."

"Of course," Peter grinned.

"Okay," Claus interrupted. "Let's get to work."

The three of them went into the massive storage area, where they found all the suitcases and clothes from last night waiting to be collected and then taken to one of the sorting rooms. They piled as much as they could possibly get onto a trolley and wheeled it to the room where the girls were waiting.

"I will show you where to go, this time," William told Peter, "but after this, you'll be on your own."

After pushing the merchandise down a long corridor, they eventually reached a room marked 'Sorting Room 10.'

"Here we are. This is your room," William told Peter. "You will always bring the things from storage to this room."

Peter took a good long look around the place. The room was about the same size as Hut 27, however, where there had been floor to ceiling bunks there; here there were four long tables with four girls sitting around each.

These girls were all sorting through the clothes and seeing which could be taken apart and used again, making clothes or blankets for the soldiers at the front line. At the same time, the girls were going through the pockets to make sure there were no hidden gems contained within. All the time they toiled, there was a female SS guard watching over them.

Peter suddenly became quite shy. He'd always been a little bashful when in the company of girls, and now to be the only man in the room (apart from William – this time,) he felt himself beginning to blush.

The girls all looked well nourished. For the past few weeks he'd gotten used to seeing men looking like skeletons walking around the compound, looking as though the very effort of moving was almost too much for them, but these girls looked good.

They were a range of ages, some not really girls but women. They ranged in age from around sixteen, Peter's age, to what he estimated to be about forty.

Some of them looked very pretty, and unlike most of the prisoners he'd seen during his stay, these women had quite good heads of hair. If they'd been shaved upon arrival, they must have been here for a good few months already for it to have grown back.

He caught the eye of one young girl, a pretty, blond haired girl with big blue eyes that looked like pools of water.

Instantly, as their eyes met, she smiled at him. He felt a fluttering in his stomach and his heart missed a beat. Could this be a feeling of love at first sight? If it was, it was something he'd never felt before.

This girl was beautiful. With her shiny long blonde hair and those piercing moist blue eyes, she was simply a vision of beauty. Peter thought she was the most beautiful girl he'd ever seen. She was an angel sent from Heaven, sent to rescue him from this Hell.

He'd obviously been smitten, but felt sad by the circumstances in which he now found himself immersed in. He wished he could have met her somewhere else, anywhere but here in this death camp.

At least now, he had a reason to look forward to his work every day, as well as having a very good reason to stay alive.

He knew that from this day forward, he was going to enjoy working here in Kanada.

# CHAPTER 7
# AN INTRODUCTION

Peter had now been working in Kanada for a good few weeks. Having been searched a couple of times in his first two or three weeks with nothing being found, (as he'd not stolen anything,) he now felt trusted, or as trusted as anyone could feel when living amongst the Nazis.

The day he'd began working for the Kanada Kommando was the day he also moved into the barracks within the building. There were two huts for the 'clean up' squad to sleep in, as well as one hut almost next door, where members of the SS assigned to Kanada, were also billeted.

Although a little scary being constantly close to the very people who wanted him dead, the good thing about this arrangement was that at night, Peter could hear music coming from the quarters of the SS. He also heard their drunken antics most nights when they relaxed, sometimes a little too much.

Young Peter was constantly worried that a drunken SS guard might wander into his room and start firing indiscriminately at the occupants, just for the guard's own amusement.

The women who worked in the sorting rooms had their own section within Kanada where they lived, but it was against the rules for males and females to socialise within the building after the working day was done, although they had permission to mingle outside after work and on a Sunday, the one free day.

On that first day at his new place of work, his day was tinged with sadness. All day long, even when looking at the beautiful girl in the sorting room he was thinking about his friend, Franz, and his impending death, later that day.

He made a conscious decision there and then that he would not become so close with any prisoners again, as it was too hard to say goodbye when inevitably they were taken away from him, but later during that first day, he'd seen that girl who'd tugged at his heart strings and made his stomach feel so strange. What an extraordinarily bad day for him to fall in love for the first time in his life.

Every time he entered the sorting room, the girl and he smiled at each other. It seemed that she was just as shy as he was. It took Peter two weeks to even say 'Hello,' but this act of politeness was immediately followed by the female officer ordering them to, "Stop fraternizing" and get on with their work.

It seemed as though the poor lad just couldn't win. However, during the next few weeks, even the guard seemed to warm to him. He may have been a Jew, but he was also a very nice, pleasant, and very polite young man.

Now, as he passed the items previously belonging to the new arrivals to the beautiful girl, they took a little longer for the exchange. He even noticed the SS officer sometimes had a slight smile on her face. However, one day the inevitable happened and all this changed.

For a few days now, he'd had a weird feeling that he was being watched but couldn't understand why. In his own mind, he'd done nothing to attract attention and had definitely not stolen anything. He'd not even been searched for more than three weeks now, so why would they be watching him? Then one day, it all came to a head.

As he entered the sorting room, as per usual, he smiled at the girl, but then he noticed the man standing in the doorway, the man he feared more than any other man in the world - Heinz Kappler!

The SS officer entered the sorting room and gave Peter a stern look, which almost froze him to the spot.

"Jew Boy, why do you spend so much time in this area?" he questioned with anger in his voice. "Is there something which fascinates you here in this room?"

He looked around at the women stripping the belongings from the new arrivals' clothing and belongings, and then continued with his interrogation.

"Oh I think you like one of these lovely ladies. Jew Boy, is this the case? Is my assumption correct? Have you fallen in love with one of these delightful young ladies?" Heinz Kappler demanded.

Peter did not raise his eyes to look at the officer, as this would have been suicidal. He just continued to study the floor. He did not answer Heinz Kappler's question, as to do so could have brought disastrous consequences.

"Do you like one of these lovely ladies, Jew Boy?" Kappler repeated sternly.

He approached the tables where the sixteen women looked petrified, but also, like Peter, tried not to catch Kappler's eye.

"Is it this girl?" Kappler asked, tapping one of the girls on the shoulder. "Look at me, Jew Boy, I asked you a question." Peter had no choice now but to look at his captor.

How he hated this man. One year ago, he was a normal young man, a young boy in fact who didn't have an ounce of hatred inside him, a young man with only love in his heart and not an enemy in the world. But now, through no fault of his own he was here, surrounded by people with guns, who hated him so much that they would have willingly put a bullet between his eyes.

What had he done to earn their hatred? The only crime he'd committed was to have been born into a Jewish family.

Even so, he was not even a great believer in the faith, so why should these people hate him so?

"Is it this girl?" Kappler demanded again, tapping another 'suspect' on the shoulder. "Answer me, Jew Boy, or I will have her taken to the wall and shot!"

"No Sir, it's not her," Peter confessed, seeing the expression of horror on the poor girl's face. He then without realising gave a quick glance at the pretty, young blonde haired girl, and Kappler pounced!

"What is your name, girl?" he questioned, dragging her from her seat at the table up to her feet.

"I am two-three-three-one-two," the terrified girl replied, obviously petrified beyond belief, and truly fearing for her life.

"I asked for your name, not your number," Heinz Kappler shouted, at the same time banging his fist on the table. "What is your name?"

"Margo,"

"Margo, what," Kappler demanded.

"Margo Koval," she trembled.

"Come with me, Margo Koval," he ordered, lifting the girl by the arm and leading her in the direction of the waiting Peter.

"Jew Boy, this lovely young lady is Margo Koval," Kappler snarled. "I think you like her, don't you?" He looked directly into the youngster's eyes and demanded again, "Do you like her, Jew Boy?"

Peter didn't know what to say, having been placed into an almost impossible situation. If he admitted that he liked her, there was a good chance she'd be executed just to spite him. If he told Heinz Kappler that he did NOT like her, then she would be executed for certain.

"Do you like her or not, Jew Boy?" he shouted again, this time even more angrily. "Tell me – Yes or no!"

"Yes," Peter said quietly, fearing the worst.

"Well then, Jew Boy let me introduce you. This is Lovely Margo," he announced, in a weird, playful mood. "Do you think she is beautiful, Jew Boy?"

"Yes Sir," Peter replied. What else could he do now?

"Would you like to see her?" Kappler questioned.

"I don't know what you mean, Sir," Peter replied with honesty.

"Do you wish to see her, Jew Boy?" he repeated. "It's a simple enough question." He looked at Peter's face and then turned to the girl. "Okay Margo Koval, undo your uniform at the top and take it off. Jew Boy wants to see you."

A look of horror came across Margo's face, as the realization of the situation dawned upon her. Peter looked at her and mouthed, 'I'm sorry' to her as she slowly undid her buttons.

"Are you shy, Lovely Margo?" Heinz Kappler said, more of a suggestion than a question.

"Yes," the young girl answered quietly, trying to suppress a sob.

"You – You Jewesses," Kappler roared at the other girls in Kanada. "Lovely Margo is shy, so you must all turn away so you cannot see her. Let me tell you, if anyone turns to look at Margo, it will be the final thing you ever do, or see in this life. Do you understand?"

This was followed by quiet murmurings of girls who were not sure whether this question should, or should not, be answered. They all did as ordered and turned to face the opposite wall as Kappler turned his attentions back toward Margo.

"You see, Lovely Margo, you see how I look after you? You see how I take care to hide your blushes. I am not a monster after all, am I?" He then moved closer and was face to face with the girl, almost touching her, nose to nose. "Do you think I'm a monster, Lovely Margo?" he demanded sinisterly.

"No Sir," the young girl lied. He'd been so close to her that she could smell the garlic sausage on his breath that he'd eaten for breakfast that morning.

As Kappler pulled away, he looked down and took a glance at her breasts.

"Look at her," he ordered Peter. "What do you think, Jew Boy?" he smiled disturbingly. "Lovely Margo has very nice breasts. Don't you think so?"

"Yes Sir," the captive Peter agreed. Again, what else could he do or say?

"Do you think her breasts are beautiful?" Kappler asked of the lad.

"Yes Sir," Peter replied.

"You may touch them," Heinz Kappler ordered.

This both disgusted and devastated Peter, as this was not a choice he should be allowed to make. The person allowed to touch the breasts of a young woman should always be the choice of the girl, and only to have them touched with her express permission.

He looked at Kappler, who could see the pain in his eyes. Peter could see that Kappler was enjoying this.

"Touch her breasts, Jew Boy, or I will take her outside now and have her shot! In fact, I will shoot her myself and you will be forced to watch! You will be responsible for, and guilty of her death!" Kappler was raging now and Peter knew this was no longer some kind of sadistic game.

"Do it," Margo pleaded. "Please, just do it. I don't mind."

"You see, Jew Boy," Kappler sneered. "Lovely Margo wants you to touch her breasts. She likes you. She yearns for you to touch her breasts. Touch them – NOW!"

Peter did as was told, and gently caressed the breasts of this beautiful young Polish girl, instantly feeling remorse for these actions of which he had no control.

"Are they nice, Jew Boy?" Kappler interrogated. "Do they feel good in your hands? Do they feel soft, yet firm and feminine?" Peter did not answer this question.

"Squeeze them hard!" the brut ordered. "Squeeze then hard and pinch her nipples. Pinch them hard enough to hurt Lovely Margo. I want you to squeeze them hard and make her scream!"

Once again, Peter mouthed "Sorry" to the girl as he did what was ordered of him. She in turn gave him the sweetest smile, as though confirming that if anyone had been ordered to perform this act of degradation upon her, she was glad it was Peter.

"Okay, that's enough, Jew Boy. I think you're enjoying it too much," Kappler snapped. "Did you enjoy touching Lovely Margo's breasts?"

"Yes Sir, very much so," he replied. Again, he had no choice. It was the only reply acceptable.

"And you, Lovely Margo," Kappler said, turning his attention to the beautiful girl. "Did you enjoy the attention given to you by this fine young man?"

"Yes Sir," she replied, although an untruth.

"Good. Then everyone is happy," Heinz Kappler laughed. "You may get dressed now, Lovely Margo and return to your table, and you Jewesses, turn back around now and get back to work immediately. You, Jew Boy, you get on with whatever it is that you do around here."

With this said, Heinz Kappler slowly walked out of Kanada Sorting Room 10 and everyone breathed a huge sigh of relief.

"I am so sorry, Margo," Peter said. "I feel dreadful!"

65

"Don't feel bad," she reassured him and gave him a kiss on the cheek. "You are a lovely, wonderful young man. But now you have the advantage."

"Whatever do you mean?" Peter asked curiously.

"You know my name is Margo, but I have no idea of yours. What is your name?" she asked, giving Peter a smile that he would remember for the rest of his life.

"It's Peter," he told her, returning the smile. "Peter Florea."

"I am very pleased to meet you, Peter Florea," she smiled, gently touching the back of his hand.

"And I am really pleased to have met you," Peter replied with total honesty.

It was obvious he was now very much in love with this girl. For the very first time in his life, he was smitten.

# CHAPTER 8
# CHRISTMAS 1943

Over the coming weeks, Margo and Peter lived for Sundays to come around. Every Sunday afternoon they met up in the main square to listen to the camp orchestra play the wonderful classical music. They'd stand side by side for an hour or so and in their minds, they imagined being transported to better times and a better place.

Although occasionally their hands touched, they tried as best as they could not to make it obvious that they were now in love with each other. This would have given Heinz Kappler and his 'murder squad' even more ammunition needed to make their lives even more of a living hell than it was already.

After the second Sunday, when they met again at the concert, now feeling more confident and not so self conscious when together, Peter took Margo to Hut 44 to meet his gypsy friends. He'd already told her about Franz, and how he'd lost his life on the very day he'd met her, and now he wanted to introduce her to Oswald and his gypsy family.

"I would love to meet them," she told Peter. "If they are your friends, they must be wonderful people."

The funny thing was, because Margo was the first girlfriend he'd ever had, although he'd lost all shyness now when with her, he felt almost embarrassed to introduce her to his friends. As he entered Hut 44, he could feel the blood rushing to his face.

"Peter my friend, how are you?" It was Oswald. He approached and hugged him. "Are you feeling okay, Peter? You are looking very red in the face."

"Oswald, I would like to introduce you to my friend, Margo," Peter announced. Oswald now understood the reason for his blushes, finding it charming.

"Your friend, or your girlfriend?" he teased, seeing the lad's embarrassment. After no reply and a few seconds of silence, Oswald turned to look at Margo.

"Enchanted my dear," he announced. "I am very pleased to meet you. I just wish it could be under better circumstances."

"Me too," Margo agreed.

"Talking about better circumstances," Peter began. "How is your friend, Lemmie?"

"He's over there," Oswald pointed to the corner of the room. "Come," he gestured, and the three walked to the man in the corner.

Peter was very happy to see that Lemmie was still alive. When they reached him, he discovered that although blind in his left eye, a little vision had returned in his right. Although still blurry, it was in the opinion of the SS, enough to keep him alive.

"What happened to Lemmie," Margo asked Peter later, as they walked back to Kanada.

"Mengele," was Peter's one word answer.

"The Beast of Auschwitz," Margo exclaimed.

"Yes, the Bastard!" Peter stated, to which Margo nodded in agreement.

They returned to the 'Gypsy Camp' the following Sunday afternoon. This had now become a regular occurrence. When the two were due to leave, Oscar had a surprise for them.

"Will you be here next Saturday?" he asked the two.

"Saturday?" a confused Peter queried.

"Yes," Oscar confirmed. "Don't you remember? It's Christmas day and we're having a party."

"Having a party?" Peter asked suspiciously.

"Well, as much of a party as possible without alcohol," Oswald confirmed. "It'll be more of a dance really."

"But how can we have music without a record player or a radio?" Peter scoffed.

"Peter my friend," Oswald started, "where do you go every Sunday? What do you listen to?"

"The orchestra," Peter answered.

"That's right," Oswald agreed, "and we have three girls who play the violin in the orchestra string section who will come here and play for us, but music we can dance to. Hopefully they might bring more of the musicians here to play for us."

"Sounds great," Peter said, now quite excited by the prospect of a party, especially as he hadn't even realised it was Christmas.

It turned out that there were never any arrivals from Christmas Eve until the day after Boxing Day, so everyone had a three day holiday. This was obviously more for the benefit of the guards, but of course, it also meant a welcome break for the prisoners.

"You will be able to relax, Peter. No one is gassed at Christmas, and no one is sent to the ovens except for the turkey," Oswald joked. As he said this almost everyone in Hut 44 burst into fits of laughter, the likes of which, Peter hadn't heard for a very long time.

Being Monday it was back to work the next day, however the atmosphere about the place seemed different somehow. The guards all seemed happier today, maybe because they knew they had a three day holiday at the end of the week to look forward to. Because of this, they all seemed far more relaxed than normal.

For some reason, as he pushed his trolley load of belongings today, Peter's eyes were drawn towards a wonderful and luxurious fur coat on the top of the pile.

He thought of the woman it once belonged to, now dead of course, and thought how she must have been a very rich and well respected member of her community, until Adolph Hitler had taken all this away!

He looked around to see if anyone was looking but they were not, so he put his hand inside the pockets to check if any valuables were hiding there. He could not believe it when he felt a large stone at the tips of his fingers. Checking again to make absolutely sure he was not being observed – again he was not – he pulled his hand out of the pocket and found ensconced within it, the biggest diamond he'd ever seen in his life! He couldn't believe his eyes when he looked at the beautiful stone, sparking even in the dim light of the corridor he was now making his way along.

What should he do, he was in two minds? If caught with this item, he would more than likely be put to death. On the other hand, if he was able to hide it for the duration of captivity it would be enough to setup Margo and he in civilian life, should that day ever come.

Taking no more chances and giving it no more thought in case he talked himself out of it, he quickly popped the diamond into his mouth and swallowed, hoping the sharpness of the edges of the precious gem would do no harm to his intestines.

For the rest of the day, as he worked he searched for a good hiding place, thinking the best place to hide his new stash would be somewhere within plain sight.

It was two days later when the gem re-emerged. Although what he needed to do to recover it had been disgusting, just looking at it again nestled in the palm of his hand was really quite something. It made his heart sing to think of the good it

70

could do for him and Margo in the future – That is if they had a future.

He'd found a hiding place at the side of the Kanada building, the one place where he could not be seen from the lookout post. If there were no guards in view, he could be there and back in a matter seconds, thirty at the most. He would do this in the morning, because no one would ever think he would be carrying stolen merchandise at the beginning of the working day and not at the end.

Eventually the time had come, but he could not believe how nervous he was. He left his living quarters with the diamond back in his mouth, just in case he was challenged, when he could swallow it again if necessary. The most disgusting thing about this was the fact that he'd not been able to give it a complete clean, so there were still deposits of his excrement on it. However, he was comforted to know that at least it was his shit and no one else's!

All around the camp, the various roll calls were taking place. Being now in the Kanada Kommando, he had no need to take part in this morning ritual, so thought this would be a great time to hide the booty.

He wandered through the main door to the outside world and meandered to the end of the frontage. Taking a good look round he couldn't see any guards approaching, so quickly went down the narrow corridor between Kanada and Gas Chamber Number Five.

Just a few yards further down, he spat the diamond out on the ground, quickly bent down and made a small hole with his finger, placed the gem in the hole and rapidly covered the diamond with earth. He then found a small stone to place on top, marking the burial spot for future reference.

The entire procedure took less than twenty seconds. He smiled, congratulating himself for getting one over on the enemy, and then went about his day with renewed vigour.

Saturday the 25th of December 1943 – Christmas day arrived. With no work and no noise to wake them, everyone seemed to sleep in late today.

Peter rose and made a conscious effort to get to the water first today, so he could have a refreshingly good wash before meeting Margo later. He was excited to be spending the day in her company, although the day was also tinged with sadness for him. It was their first Christmas together, but he'd not been able to buy her a gift. He promised himself that the first Christmas they spent together in freedom; he would buy her the best present money could buy.

After the usual morning cup of slop, he made his way to the main square. He'd arranged to meet his darling there and listen with her to the orchestra playing traditional Christmas Carols.

Upon arrival, he spotted her immediately. She'd also made a special effort today to make herself more presentable than usual. Peter looked at her. Her blonde hair was shining in the midday sun. She looked so stunningly beautiful. He just wished he were able to take her in his arms and passionately kiss her.

One surreal thing about this day was the fact that there were far more guards here than on a Sunday, the usual day for a concert. However, with today being a holiday, even the guards seemed different. They were also here to celebrate the day and looked to have no interest in terrifying the inmates. In fact, the entire camp definitely had a much more relaxed atmosphere about the place today.

The music sounded quite wonderful. All the prisoners sang along to all the carols, but when the orchestra played "Stille

Nacht" – (Silent Night) – even the guards joined in, performing a duet with the prisoners and singing along with great gusto.

Two hours later, Margo and Peter arrived at Hut 44 ready for the shindig. Oswald met them with a smile.

"Hello, you two. Are you ready to let go of all inhibitions and have a good time?" he questioned.

"I hope so," replied Peter.

"Of course," Margo chipped in.

The place looked almost the same as usual, but as they had permission from the guards to have this get-together they had been supplied with a few wooden planks with which they'd constructed a small stage in the corner of the room. So what if the wood had come from the crematorium next door? Today was not a day to dwell on the present situation, but was a day to have fun.

"Looking good," Peter observed, looking around the hut.

"It's the one good thing about working in construction," Oswald replied.

They sat about chatting until the three girls from the string section of the orchestra arrived armed with their violins. Even better, they'd persuaded the cellist to come along with her instrument, which she assured them could also be used to play as a double bass.

With the four of them performing and one of the gypsies, Patrick, improvising with a couple of small wooden boxes for drums, they were ready. Very soon, the dancing would begin.

Again, in his head Peter used the word, surreal. It was surreal to see the girls he watched every Sunday afternoon now standing (they were normally seated) and dancing as they played, not sombre but beautiful classical music, they now played a type of Wild West American barn dance style of music.

Everyone was soon having a wild time, shrieking and in howls of laughter. Even Peter and his beautiful friend joined in, spinning round and around on the make shift dance floor.

"Are you having fun," Peter questioned his beautiful friend.

"So much," confirmed Margo. "I love being with you. I love being anywhere with you," she said and kissed him on the cheek.

"Careful," Peter warned, scared of being seen by the wrong type of people.

"Sorry, but I just wanted to kiss you," Margo admitted smiling. "It is Christmas Day, after all."

"Margo, I promise you we will have many more Christmas Days to come, and all better than this one," said Peter.

"Don't promise me that, Peter," Margo sighed. "We could both be dead before the next one!"

Suddenly the door to the hut opened and an SS guard entered, but without making any sound or giving any orders, he just stood and watched everyone enjoying themselves. Oswald saw the officer and walked slowly towards him.

"Is everything okay, Sir?" he questioned. "We do have permission to have this party today."

"No-No-No," the officer replied. "I've not come in here to cause any problems for you. I heard the music and came in to listen. Do you mind?"

"Of course not, Sir," Oscar replied, wondering if this could be a test. "You are more than welcome to stay."

"Thank you," replied the SS man, who then very curiously saluted Oswald. "Carry on everyone. Don't mind me. Please, you have a good time and Merry Christmas to you all."

Peter was still very suspicious, as he'd never seen this young man before, for that's what he was, a young man, who could only have been twenty-two or three, if he was a day.

He spent the next few minutes watching him closely, but soon realised he was no problem for them – today! In fact, the young man was soon seen tapping his foot in time with the music. One of the gypsy girls even plucked up the courage to ask him to dance with her.

"I would love to," he replied with honesty, "but if my superior officer came in and found me fraternising with the 'enemy,' I'd more than likely be locked up in here with you."

"Oh! That would never do!" the girl said sarcastically. The officer gave her a sympathetic smile, almost apologetic.

He stayed for more than an hour and was no problem at all. Margo studied him and thought that he looked like he really wanted to join in with the fun. He also looked as if he had no hatred for these people.

It was a well known fact that not all the guards in Auschwitz Birkenau were Jew or Gypsy haters, but were just following orders. Margo was convinced that this young man was one of the 'good guys.'

Tuesday the 27$^{th}$ of December 1943, the day after Boxing Day, the holiday was well and truly over and the camp returned to normal. Even the habitual scowls were back, etched upon the faces of the guards as they returned to work, their work of terrorising the inmates.

# CHAPTER 9
# HAUS VON KAPPLER
(House of Kappler)

Heinz Kappler was born, raised, and lived all his life in the beautiful city of Munich. His childhood was that of a perfectly normal young man, going to a normal school, playing football with friends in the park, going to the cinema and chatting to girls with the hope of taking the relationships a little further.

He didn't care about the race of these people, black or white, rich, poor, or even Jewish, he only thought about them being good or bad, beautiful or not so. However, in his later teens, he discovered a social life taking place in the many bier halls of Munich.

When he was in his early twenties, he heard about this strange man who was kicking up a storm with his speeches, so decided to attend one to see what all the fuss was about. He popped along to attend one of these meetings, a gathering taking place in the upstairs drinking hall of the famous, Hofbräuhaus Bierkeller, situated just off the Marienplatz and close to the Munich city centre.

He watched in an almost hypnotic state as this almost insignificant little man had an audience of more than three hundred men whipped up into a state of frenzy. They began banging their fists on the table, but by the end of his speech, they were actually standing on the tables and stamping their feet in support. The name of this man of course, was Adolph Hitler, and he was about to change the world.

Heinz Kappler was mesmerised by this man and was soon attending these meetings regularly. Spotted by Hitler himself at one of these meetings, he was later taken under his wing.

Soon the two men were good friends, sharing the odd stein of pilsner or two at the end of the meetings, and when invited, Kappler was more than willing to join Hitler's Nazi party.

Before long, the younger man shared the same total hatred of the Jews and agreed with his friend, Adolph that these people must be removed from the face of the earth and must be erased from history!

A few years later, when the camps of Auschwitz One and Auschwitz Birkenau were constructed to help with the 'Final Solution," Heinz Kappler jumped at the chance to be a part of the set-up when personally invited by the Fuehrer himself.

Although not the top man in the camp, that distinction fell to Rudolph Höss, Kappler was still a high ranking officer, considered to be a much valued component and very important to the killing machine.

It was now March 1944. Although the nights were still on the cold side, daytime temperatures were rising. When the sun shone, it could be reasonably warm.

Peter, now well established in the Kanada Kommando had committed his act of theft a further five times, and had now built up a decent stash buried outside the Kanada complex, all in the same spot and covered by the one single stone.

He had no problem sleeping at night, as in the very unlikely event that his collection of jewels was ever discovered, there was no way of knowing or proving that he was the culprit.

There had been a weird feeling around the camp now for a few weeks, with far more new arrivals coming every day. It was as though there was a rush to finish off all the unwanted 'filth' quickly and send them to their makers. For this reason, Peter's work in the Kanada Kommando had been even busier than usual.

The good thing about this was the fact that he was able to be in the company of Margo for longer each day. Even though they'd still spent no private time alone together, with definitely no moments of intimacy, their love for each other was still growing stronger, each and every day.

How he longed to take her in his arms and squeeze every last drop of breath out of her body, then give her the biggest kiss he could muster. Peter hoped this dream would come true very soon, one day in the not too distant future.

As he pushed the trolley load of clothes and belongings in through the entrance to the sorting room, the girls all looked up at him.

"Good morning ladies," he said smiling.

"Two-Nine-Eight-Six-One, be quiet," ordered the female officer.

"Sorry Mam," he said looking in her direction. He noticed her trying to stifle a smile. He was sure she was one of the good ones.

"Get on with your work, Two-Nine-Eight-Six-One," the guard demanded.

'Two-Nine-Eight-Six-One is so formal,' he thought to himself. 'I do wish she'd just call me - Two.'

He afforded himself a little chuckle, which thankfully she didn't notice. He did however notice the large figure looming at the entrance to the room and making the hairs on the back of his neck stand on end when he realised it was Heinz Kappler.

"Jew Boy, you are here again," he observed, as the room fell into total silence.

"I do work here, Sir," Peter replied, instantly regretting saying it. Kappler just gave him a look that could kill – literally.

"Well, Jew Boy, tomorrow you will not be working here," he said, intensifying the stare. "You must report to the Administration Block first thing in the morning."

When Kappler had left the room, Peter looked at Margo. "What does he need you for?" she questioned.

"I don't know," Peter replied. "But it can't be good."

After a restless night of tossing and turning, the next morning, as requested, Peter walked through the entrance of the Admin Block as ordered.

"Number," the man at the desk asked indignantly.

"Two-Nine-Eight-Six-One," Peter replied.

"Well, Two-Nine-Eight-Six-One, you are going to the house of SS Officer Heinz Kappler. He needs you to do something for him."

"Do something for him?" Peter gasped. "What can I possibly do for him?"

"You will find out soon," the man seated at the desk laughed. "Go outside now and there is transport waiting to take you."

This phrasing scared him to death. The last time he'd been ordered to take the 'transport,' he'd ended up with a two day journey, culminating in his arrival here.

As he left the building, he was relieved to see the waiting car. He was walking towards it when a Sonderkommando came up to him. "Have a nice day," he laughed. This made Peter feel even more uneasy. What did these people know that he didn't?

Positioning himself inside on the back seat of the waiting car, he noticed the driver now waiting for him. He immediately realized that this was the same guard who he'd seen at the Christmas Day party in Hut 44, the Christmas party held at the Gypsy block.

"So, you are working today at the house of SS Officer Kappler," the driver announced.

"Yes," replied Peter. "But I have no idea why, or what he wants me to do."

"Relax," the young guard told him, whilst turning to face him. "If you were going to die today it would be done here in the camp. Heinz Kappler is not going to shoot you in his home in front of his wife and children," he laughed.

Peter had never thought of Kappler as being a family man. What this young guard had said to him reassured him - slightly.

"What is your name?" the young blond haired guard questioned.

"I am Two-Nine-Eight-Six-One, Sir," Peter replied.

"No," he laughed. "What is your name? What did your mother call you?"

"I am Peter, Peter Florea."

"I am pleased to meet you, Peter. It's a shame it could not be under better circumstances," he said sincerely. 'Why did everyone say this?' Peter asked himself, 'Did no one really want to be here in this place?'

"My name is Paul – Paul Fuster," he informed the youngster. "Please believe me when I tell you that I do not want to be here in Auschwitz any more than you do." He then went on to tell Peter a little about himself.

Paul Fuster was born and lived most of his life in a little, medieval town called, Peina, situated in the north of Germany, close to Hannover.

He was a very nice young man; everyone who knew him always said so. With his mop of blond hair and blue eyes, along with an athletic figure, he was extremely good looking and a big hit with the girls. He had the type of Arian features of which the Fuhrer desired, but this was something he hated, especially when his friends teased him about it.

"When we win the war, Heir Adolph will use you for the breeding programme," his friends often joked, but they had no idea how much this revolted him.

The very name of Hitler repulsed him, he despised the man and his ideas, but to admit this would have been no good for either him or his family.

Even in these troubled times he tried to live life as normally as possible. He would often be found surrounded by friends, both male and 'adoring' females, in his local hostelry, 'The Black Swan,' situated in the Peina Market Place. Here they would consume copious amounts of the local brew, Harke Bier, just as any other group of young friends would do in normal times – But these were NOT normal times – there was a war raging.

Paul loathed the fact that his country was at war, especially with Britain. He had not an ounce of hatred in his body for anyone, or any race in the world.

Ten years earlier when he was ten or eleven years of age, it would have been around 1933 when his parents actually took him to the south of England for a brief holiday. He remembered how idyllic life had been in those days.

He'd made sandcastles on the beach at Weymouth and enjoyed afternoon tea, freshly baked scones with strawberry jam and clotted cream. He remembered it as a beautiful place, so how could the Fatherland now want to destroy the country he remembered so fondly, along with the people who were so polite to him and his parents?

He was also sure that he even had some distant English cousins, but this was something he did not brag about or broadcast to anyone, not even his best friends.

Paul had been in his final year of a law degree at university in Hannover when he received notice to attend an army recruitment center. This angered him and he rightly or wrongly made his displeasure known at training camp. He even let it be known that he had absolutely no intention of killing anyone he couldn't see face to face. Why should he, unless they posed a personal threat or danger to him?

"The only reason they are there in the opposite trench to me is because someone hundreds of miles away from the front line had ordered them to be there," he claimed at training camp. This did not make him a very popular man.

As a type of conscientious objector, he'd been given the choice of two options, option one was to stand against a wall and face a firing squad, or he could take option two and be sent to Auschwitz to be a guard. He'd chosen option two, although he had no idea of what this job entailed.

When he'd first arrived at the camp, he was placed in the lookout post, but it soon became obvious to those higher up that he would not fire his gun at anyone if called upon to take action.

He was ordered to see Heinz Kappler, who for some extraordinary reason, liked the young man, took pity on him and had made him his personal driver, a few months back.


"So what would you do if I jumped out of the car and made a run for it?" Peter questioned. "Would you shoot me?"

"I'll tell you what would happen," Fuster began. He pulled the car over and stopped before continuing and getting serious.

"Yes, I would shoot at you. The fact is, if you escaped from me it would be my fault, and Kappler would put a bullet between my eyes before the day was finished.

If you were successful and got away, all your Gypsy friends would be sent to the gas chamber tomorrow, except for Oswald and Margo."

"Margo!" Peter gushed.

"Yes Margo," Fuster confirmed. "Kappler knows how you feel about the two of them, especially Margo. They would be sent to the Gestapo and tortured for a few days before being hanged in the main square. They would make all the prisoners watch them hang as a warning for them not to attempt an escape. If you get away but they catch you, you would hang with them. The last thing you would ever see in this world would be the girl you love, hanging by the neck until she's dead."

"The girl I love?" Peter asked cautiously. The guard laughed.

"Of course," Fuster replied. "Do you think the guards are blind? They all know of the love building between the two of you."

Hearing this, Peter was apprehensive. "Am I putting Margo's life in danger by showing her all the daily attention?" he questioned Fuster.

"Don't worry, my friend. If they were going to take any offence, they would have dealt with you before now."

"And Kappler, does he know?" Peter asked cautiously.

"Especially Kappler," Fuster acknowledged. "For some reason he likes you, maybe something to do with you volunteering to come here to Auschwitz Birkenau?"

"He knows about that?" Peter asked, not knowing how he felt about it.

"Peter, Heinz Kappler knows everything," was Paul Fuster's final word on the subject, as they finally arrived at a very smart house in the country.

Peter estimated by the time taken to drive here that it was about ten miles from the camp, far enough he thought to protect Kappler's two children from the horrors of what their father really did for a living.

As Paul Fuster led him up the garden path, Peter could feel his legs turning to jelly and he began to shake with fear. This is how much Heinz Kappler scared the shit out of him! He then remembered and took comfort in what Fuster had said to him on the journey.

"If you are going to die today, you will die in the camp and not in the house of Kappler."

Peter took a sharp intake of breath to give him courage, as Paul Fuster knocked on the door. The door was opened by a strikingly, good looking woman.

"Can I help you?" she questioned.

"Can you please tell Officer Kappler that the worker is here?" Fuster requested. After saying this, he returned to the car, telling Peter he'd be waiting outside when his work was finished.

"Oh, please come in," the woman said to Peter, opening the door for him.

Stepping inside, he took a good look at her. She was in her mid thirties and very pretty. He wondered what on Earth she was doing with a monster like Kappler. In the corner of the room, he spotted a young boy of about six years of age playing with a toy car. Peter thought how normal he looked.

"Adolph, say hello to the worker," the woman said to her son.

Peter nearly choked when hearing this. Mein Gott! Kappler even named his son after the Fuhrer! How more fanatical could he get?

"Heinz is in the viewing room," the woman said. "He said for you to go in when you arrive."

She pointed the way and Peter walked along the corridor in the direction she'd pointed. He tried to walk as slowly as possible to delay the inevitability of what he thought might happen. Reaching the door, he tapped on it as quietly as possible.

"Come," he heard the voice say and recognised it immediately. Instantly the butterflies in his stomach began performing a merry dance.

Entering the room, he was confronted by a bizarre sight. The room was almost in darkness and Kappler was sitting in a large, comfortable looking armchair, in the middle of the room but with his back to the lad. A few feet in front of him was a large movie screen and the clickety-click sound of a machine projecting the image onto the screen could be heard. However, the most surreal thing about all this was when he heard Kappler laughing.

"Ah, you are here – Good," he said, but he said it quietly, not like the angry, abrupt manner he used in the camp, this was, well, normal. "Tell me boy, do you like Charlie Chaplin?" It was then that Peter realised he was watching a Chaplin movie. "His little tramp is so funny," Kappler said, laughing again.

"Yes, I think he's very funny, Sir," Peter answered.

"Good," Kappler muttered. He stood up to look at Peter. "I expect you're wondering why you are here," he suggested.

"Yes Sir," Peter answered, taking a good look at the man now standing before him.

Heinz Kappler was dressed in an immaculate white silk shirt that was open at the top two buttons, sharply pressed cream slacks with turn-ups at the bottom of each leg, and he wore highly polished brown, brogue style shoes. Peter thought he looked much smaller in civvies than he did in the scary SS uniform he'd always seen him wearing at the camp, and yes, very much less intimidating.

Kappler looked at the lad and continued. "I remembered that when you first arrived on the transport, you told me you were an engineer," he reminded the lad.

"No Sir," Peter lied, thinking quickly. "I told you I was studying to be an engineer."

"Fair enough," Kappler conceded. "I have brought you here because I want you to build an extension to the kitchen at the back of the house. Would this be a problem for you?"

He stared at Peter whilst the youngster, now in a total state of panic, churned over in his mind what could be the answer, but then Kappler began to laugh loudly.

"Jew Boy, do you think I am stupid?" he questioned without raising his voice. "The day you arrived, I knew you were no more an engineer than I am a belly dancer! You are here simply because my wife keeps asking about my work at the camp. She has wanted such a long time to meet one of you people living there. She thinks, as you did when you first arrived, that it is a work camp. Answer her questions, but if you divulge the truth about the killings, Margo, your Margo will be placed on the list and sent to the gas chamber. Do we understand each other?"

"Yes Sir," Peter conceded.

"Now, so we have a reason for you to be here you can do some work tidying the garden," Kappler ordered. "You can start by cutting the grass, and when you finish, come back and I'll find something else for you to do. But if my wife comes and speaks with you, well, just remember your Lovely Margo."

Later as he mowed the lawn, Kappler's wife came out to see him. "I've brought you a cup of tea and a sandwich," she announced.

Peter wondered if this was some kind of trick. He really hesitated when she invited him to sit in the comfortable garden chair and chat for a while. He took a sip of the tea and tasted something for the first time in almost six months.

"I'm sorry, I should have asked, would you like sugar with your tea?" Mrs. Kappler queried.

"No," Peter replied. "No thank you, Mam."

"Please, call me Christa," the lady of the house requested. Again, Peter wondered if this could be another test.

"I'd rather not," he replied. Then thinking quickly, he said, "I'd rather call you 'Mam' out of respect for you and your husband."

Inwardly he smiled to himself. If this was all a test, he thought he was doing okay so far.

"What is my husband like to work for?" she questioned. Again, Peter thought long and hard before answering.

"He is a fair man," he lied. "If you work hard, he will look after you. However, he does not like slackers. He has no time for them."

"And is the food good in the camp? Is the café' and food hall of a decent standard?"

Christa Kappler looked really sweet and lovely as she asked this question, but Peter could not believe how naive she was. Did she truly not know why the family were living here? Did she truly not know the kind of monster her husband was, or about the 'death camp' he was involved in the running of?

He actually began feeling sorry for her and the children. One day when the truth came out, the bubble would burst and she'd be devastated.

Before he answered her question, he bit his lip firmly and thought about Margo's future safety.

"Officer Kappler is a good boss and always makes sure we finish work before the café' closes, so we can get a hot meal at the end of the working day. The food is always good, well cooked and a good variety is offered, different every day." He almost felt sick when telling these lies.

Christa offered him a sandwich. "It's not much," she said, "just ham and cheese."

She had no idea of how Peter was salivating at the thought of this tasty treat, but the young man couldn't decide whether he should accept it? He finally gave in.

"Lovely," he said, extending his arm to accept the plate of food. The first bite was divine, and he savoured every morsel.

"What is your name?" she questioned.

"With respect, Mam, I don't know if I should answer that question," he replied. She looked confused so Peter elaborated. "There are so many of us working at the camp that we are only known by number. My number is Two-Nine-Eight-Six-One. I don't think your husband would want me to confuse the situation by telling you my name."

"Nonsense," she said sternly. "I am NOT going to call you by a number. What is your name?"

"It's Peter," he admitted. "Peter Florea."

"Well Peter Florea, it has been lovely meeting you today."

"Thank you, Mam," he said and meant it.

He felt sorry for this lovely lady who was making him feel so welcome to her home. Whatever happened in the future, she was in for a massive shock, but he genuinely hoped she would survive.

"Mummy who is this?" a little girl asked whilst studying the man wearing striped pyjamas during the daytime. "He looks like he's dressed for bed," she laughed.

"Don't be naughty, Eva," Christa scolded the child. "This is Peter and he's come to help Daddy with some gardening."

'The children are named Eva and Adolph,' Peter thought. 'Only in the world of Heinz Kappler could his two children be named after the Fuhrer and his mistress.' He also found it difficult to accept for Kappler to be known as Daddy!

The little girl came to Peter and rested her head in his lap. Again, he did not know how to react to this.

"You smell funny," Eva exclaimed, scrunching up her little nose.

"Eva," her mother shouted. "Don't be naughty. Peter has been working hard. That's why he smells so badly."

"Oh, okay" was all the little girl said, as she shook her head and ran away.

"I'm sorry about Eva," Christa said.

"That's okay, she's only young," Peter replied.

"Would you like some more tea, or more to eat?" the lovely wife of Kappler questioned.

Peter thought better of it this time. He thought it not a good idea to abuse the situation, so refused the offer, even though he'd been starving hungry for the past six months.

He went back to work and an hour later, after finishing the lawn, a good job, even if he thought so himself, he went back to the room where Heinz Kappler was waiting. The door was open so he just walked straight in to find him sitting in the same position and watching more Chaplin movies on the screen. At first, Kappler didn't notice the boy had entered the room.

What was different now was that on a table to the side, the monster had left his belt, which held the holster for his pistol. Peter could clearly see the gun was still inside. Was this the greatest test of all? He could easily get to the gun before Kappler could react, take it out of the holster and put a bullet in the back of the monster's head.

Again, he asked himself if this was a test. If he took the gun and attempted to shoot Heinz Kappler but there were no bullets inside, the gun would be loaded and turned on him.

Should the gun contain bullets and he succeeded in killing the monster, then tomorrow, one thousand Auschwitz Jews would be sent to their deaths and he and Margo would hang in the main square and left for days for everyone to see as a deterrent. He thought better of it.

"Ah the Jew has finished his work," Kappler announced, seeing Peter was back in the room. He then spotted his gun left alone on the table.

"I know what you are thinking, Jew Boy, is the gun loaded, or not?" Peter made no reaction at this, as Kappler continued. "Well you snivelling, filthy Jew, this is something you will never know!"

So there it was, in one sentence, the real SS Officer Heinz Kappler was back in the room.

# CHAPTER 10
# THE SUMMER OF 44

Luckily, the day after the visit to Kappler's house fell on a Sunday, so Peter and Margo were able to spend some quality free time together and he was able to tell her all about the events of the previous day.

She was amazed when he told her about his chat with Christa Kappler, especially about how she honestly believed that Auschwitz Birkenau was some sort of holiday camp, whilst her husband was a well loved and respected man in the place, who looked after his 'workers very well!'

"What is she like, Peter?" Margo queried. "Is she bad like Kappler?"

"No, she's a very nice lady," Peter explained. "She is very polite and good company to be with. I honestly don't believe she has a clue what her husband is really like, or what work he does."

"She should come and spend a day here in the camp," Margo suggested. "She would soon find out what a truly lying bastard her husband, Kappler, really is!"

"Maybe she could come and join us in the games room," Peter mocked. They both laughed at the thought.

Two days later, they were back in Sorting Room 10. As usual, Peter was taking as long as possible to unload his trolley of luggage and belongings so he could spend as much time with his darling girl as possible, when they received another visit from Kappler.

"Oh Jew Boy, you are here," he said. This time Peter did not answer. "I want to congratulate you. You were a big hit with my wife and children. Adolph keeps asking when the 'worker' is returning, as he wants to play catch the ball with you."

"He's a nice boy," Peter chipped in, but this was totally ignored by Kappler.

"My wife really likes you." Kappler continued.

"She's a nice lady." Peter stated.

"Yes she is," Kappler agreed. "She likes you so much that she's asked me to invite you to dinner next Sunday, but I have told her that Sunday is your day off and you like to spend it socialising with friends, so it would not be possible for you to come to my house for dinner."

"You could always bring her here," Peter remarked sarcastically. "She could come and eat dinner with us in one of the many cafés and eateries we have here."

He instantly regretted saying this when he felt the full, ferocious force of Kappler's leather gloved right hand, as the palm of it was smacked across his face, knocking him to the ground.

"You insolent swine!" the officer snarled, and before leaving the room, he kicked Peter before he could stand.

As soon as he was gone, Margo stood up from the table and attempted to run to him, but before she could do so, the female guard stopped her.

"Two-Three-Three-One-Two sit down!" she screamed at her and Margo did as she was ordered.

She wanted to go to Peter to comfort him and kiss his cheek to make it better, like her mother did to her when she was a young child, but this bitch was stopping her from doing so. Even though Peter seemed to have a bit if a rapport for this guard, Margo still hated the woman!

"Two-Three-Three-One-Two - Get back to your work – NOW!" the guard barked again.

Peter stood up and dusted himself down. He looked at Margo and gave her a wink of his eye to let her know he was okay. She smiled in return. Peter thought it was worth the beating just to receive that smile from the girl he loved.

Later, back in the storage facility, seeing the big red mark on his cheek, William Straus came up to Peter.

"What the hell happened to you?" he demanded. Peter told him what happened earlier about Kappler hitting him. "Why did he do that?" William asked, as if Heinz Kappler needed a reason to inflict pain on anyone.

William listened, amazed when he heard the story of Peter's visit to the Kappler house. He listened intently to the story of the gun and did it have bullets or not, and paid attention to the conversation between Peter and the 'naive' Christa Kappler. He laughed when hearing the children were named Adolph and Eva, however, the anecdote which gave him the most interest, without a doubt, was the story of the 'Cheese and Ham Sandwich!'

"What did it taste like," William asked, almost slobbering like a dog. "I want you to describe every last tasty mouthful in great detail."

William listened attentively as Peter described the tasty treat, describing every morsel. William thought of the sandwich and decided that to eat one now would be better than sex. Not that he could remember what having sex was like!

Although time in the camp went by slowly, March soon turned to April and very soon, it was July 1944. The acceleration of arrivals was still in the ascendance, but what Peter also realised to his horror was that there were now a lot more people being sent to the right, and so to their deaths immediately upon arrival. Because of this, there were now fewer prisoners in the camp, and most of those who were here, through lack of food were mostly just skin and bones. The German authorities were just leaving them to die of so called, natural causes, although there was nothing natural about the deaths of these poor souls.

As there were now fewer prisoners to police, there seemed to be fewer guards on the ground, which aided Peter's decision to get back to his thieving ways and increase his stash for the future, should he ever survive and get out of this place.

The days now were very hot, making roll call just as dangerous for the men as it was in the cold and snow of the winter. Inmates were now collapsing and even dying of heat exhaustion, after being forced to stand in direct sunlight for hours at a time. Those who did die were unceremoniously loaded into trolleys and carted off to the crematorium, although some now were just left to rot where they fell!

"Let the birds feed off the scum," he once heard Kappler say.

One morning during the first week of July, the men were all standing for the roll call in the main square when a large staff car arrived. Out stepped none other than Rudolph Höss, accompanied by Heinz Kappler. Moments later, twelve Hungarian prisoners were marched into the square and ordered to stand in a line.

"These men had the audacity to think they could escape from this camp," Kappler began, after first ordering the men at roll call to pay 'close' attention. "They were wrong," he continued. "There is no escape from Auschwitz." He turned and pointed to the billowing smoke coming from the chimney of the crematorium. "That is the only way you will escape the power of the Third Reich!"

Rudolph Höss came and stood in front of the twelve escapees. They looked terrified and wondered what their punishment might be. Would they be whipped in public, with maybe one hundred lashes each? Maybe they would be tortured by the Gestapo for days on end. Sadly, they soon discovered the answer.

"Prisoners, lay face down on the ground," Rudolph Höss ordered.

As they did this, Höss looked across at Heinz Kappler and gave him a nod of the head. Kappler immediately pulled his gun from its holster and positioned himself above the first man in the line and then - BANG – the man's head splattered all over the ground.

All the remaining Hungarians became frantic upon hearing the gun go off, realising what was to be their fate. Then – BANG – all life was extinguished from the second man.

Kappler repeated this operation until reaching the ninth man. This time, when he pointed the gun at the man's head and pulled the trigger, a loud clicking sound was heard all around the camp. The following silence was unbearable!

"I am very sorry," Kappler said sarcastically to the doomed man. "It would appear that I have run out of bullets."

The poor man looked up and with pleading eyes, he watched Kappler reload the gun and then point it back towards him. BANG – BANG – BANG – BANG - the man and all three remaining men were dead, all shot mercilessly by Heinz Kappler, the murderer of Auschwitz!

Peter was in the storage facility loading up his trolley when he heard the first gunshot. He was about to go outside when William Straus ran to him.

"No Peter, don't go out there, you will get yourself shot," he demanded of the young man.

"But they are my fellow countrymen," Peter pleaded.

"And what if they are, there's nothing you can do for them," Once again, William Straus was the voice of reason.

"One day I am going to kill Heinz Kappler," Peter stated. "And that is a promise!"

"Okay," Claus said when hearing the conversation. "But not today, Peter, and not whilst you are still in this camp."

"Okay," peter agreed. "But you mark my words, as true as I'm standing here before you, one day I will find that man and I will show him no mercy. He is evil and he must die!"

# CHAPTER 11
## 'THE RETREAT'

One August morning, the girls were working hard as usual in Sorting Room 10 when a rather stern looking female guard entered the room. She shouted two numbers before shouting Margo's number.

"Two-Six-Two-Eight-one, Two-Three-Four-Seven-Eight and Two-Three-Three-One-Two, come with me."

The three young girls all looked at each other as if to say, 'where are they taking us? Why do they need us? Are they going to send us to the gas chamber?'

Once outside Kanada they could see that they were the only girls selected and there was no one else outside waiting to join them. This gave them hope, as they were sure they would not send three girls only to the gas chamber.

"Follow me," the guard ordered. "If you try to run away, I WILL shoot you," she instructed.

The girls followed as the four of them (including the guard) walked out through the entrance of Auschwitz Birkenau. For Margo, this was the first time she'd left the camp since arriving more than a year ago.

Meanwhile back in Kanada, Peter had just entered the sorting room. When he noticed Margo's empty chair, he almost collapsed.

"Where is she?" he shouted.

"Be quiet, Two-Nine-Eight-Six-One," he was ordered by the guard, the nice one.

"Where is she?" he demanded again, even more frantic by now.

"Two-Nine-Eight-Six-One, come with me," the guard instructed whilst walking toward him. She led him into an unoccupied room to the side of the sorting room.

"Where is she?" Peter pleaded again, but this time in a much calmer manner.

"What is your name – Not your number – Your name," the guard asked.

"Peter – It's Peter," he revealed.

"Well Peter, I can tell you that she's been taken away with two other girls to work elsewhere for a day or two," the officer told him.

"Work where?" Peter asked, now almost going crazy.

"I cannot tell you where – I do know, but cannot tell you," the guard admitted. "But I will tell you that she'll be perfectly safe, I promise you. She might even have some fun. Lord knows she deserves some fun after being in this place for all this time."

"I always knew you were one of the nice ones," Peter smiled.

"If you tell anyone that, I will shoot you myself," she laughed, patting the youngster on the shoulder.

After twenty minutes or so, Margo and the gang reached the entrance to another camp. As they walked through an archway, she looked up to see a sign above her head that read, "ARBEIT MACHT FREI" – "Work Makes You Free."

Immediately her thoughts went to Peter. He'd told her about this sign in the propaganda leaflets he'd read which made him want to volunteer to come to this terrible place. She also then began to panic, as she knew that this was the place where Doctor Josef Mengele performed his experimental operations. She hoped with all her might that this was not the reason for her being here this day.

The girls breathed a huge sigh of relief, as they were led passed Block 10 without stopping at 'Mengele's Hospital.'

As they passed Block 11, Margo looked at the wall linking the two blocks. This was the execution wall, where hundreds of men had been executed over the years by firing squad.

Eventually they reached their destination and Margo and the two other girls were taken inside Block 24. This was a strange looking place, Margo thought, but then she saw something even stranger. She saw young women walking around in various states of undress. These girls all looked very well. It was obvious they were very well fed and were really clean.

"What is this place?" she asked the guard.

"Why, don't you know?" the guard smiled, almost laughing. "This is the Auschwitz brothel. This is where the guards are rewarded for their hard work with an hour of sex and debauchery."

A look of sheer terror came on all three of the girls faces. "But I am a..." Margo began to say.

"NO – NO – NO! This is not why you are here," the guard said loudly. "Look at you. How would any of you know how to satisfy a man? What use would you skinny young things be to anyone in here?" The guard laughed again.

"So why are we here?" Margo dared to ask.

"This afternoon you are to be waitresses at 'The Retreat,' so you're here to get cleaned up and be made to look presentable."

"The Retreat?" another girl, Mandy questioned. "What is The Retreat?"

"You will find out when you get there. Don't worry, you will have fun," the woman in charge said to reassure them. "Now get out of these prison clothes and take a bath."

All naked now, the girls were taken into a room with a huge circular bath, big enough for all of them to easily get in together. Margo wondered what this bath would have been used for normally, but even the thoughts in her head disgusted her. However, when she felt the warmth of the water, all previous thoughts went away and she stepped in with the other two girls.

Soon they were having fun, splashing each other and laughing together. They were even given soap to wash themselves with. Margo took a big piece and lathered it up, running it through her hair. It felt so good to have cleanly washed hair again, and when the girls all took turns to scrub each other's backs, it was pure heaven.

When bath time was over, the girls were presented with luxurious towels to dry themselves with, after which they were taken to another room. Inside this room, the girls were given crisp white shirts, black knee length skirts and little white ankle socks. They were then told to select a pair of black shoes from the pile. When dressed, they were inspected by the guard.

"You'll do," she announced. "Follow me."

Again, the girls followed the female guard back into the outside world, where a waiting car was already there for them. Once again, curiosity got the better of Margo.

"Why are we dressed like this," she questioned.

"You my girl are going to a party," the woman said, but then seeing the expression on Margo's face, she quickly added, "No girls, you are not THE party. You will be waitressing at the party."

Not very long after the journey commenced, they arrived at their destination.

'The Retreat' was a place for the Auschwitz guards to come and relax as a reward for all the hard work they did in the camp. In the early years when the camp contained mainly locals, the Polish prisoners were taken into the hills close to the camp, and on the edge of a fast flowing river, it was these men who built this place. It was just like a holiday park, where twice a month the guards, both male and female, came together and just had fun away from the horrors of camp life.

Margo couldn't believe it when seeing it for the first time. It was like something out of a fairytale. It was unbelievable to think it was still inside the Auschwitz compound. It could easily have been a million miles away.

The most amazing thing for her was how different the guards looked when dressed in normal clothes. The girls were all dressed in pretty blouses and pleated skirts, and Margo thought they all looked beautiful, and so much younger than when in uniform. The men out of uniform also looked very different, quite normal and even friendly.

They were all laughing and having fun. The men were chasing the girls and the girls were allowing them to catch them. They were playing a kind of kiss chase, just like the game she used to play as a child. However, this was definitely a kiss chase for adults only!

The pretty gilrs were all in a line, sitting on a wall with their backs to a scenic forest. The young men were feeding the girls with fresh blueberries and grapes, like a scene from the Roman Coliseum.

How Margo wished she could also be sitting on this wall with these girls, but having fresh blueberries and grapes fed to her by Peter. This was possibly the worst torture she'd suffered since her imprisonment here in Auschwitz Birkenau!

Margo and the other two girls from the Kanada sorting room 10 were three of around twenty other waitresses supplying drinks to the guards and keeping their glasses topped up. She wondered if the happy atmosphere and pleasantness might turn sour, the longer the day went on and the drunker these people became.

The reason why Margo, along with the other two girls had been fetched here today was explained by the guard who'd brought them. Apparently at the last party, the revellers all complained about the slow service. They needed to get their drinks quicker to get drunk faster and have a good time.

"If you do a good job today girls, this could be a regular feature for you," they were told by the guard.

Margo thought about this, thinking that if she did a good job today it could be a good reason for her to be kept alive, so no matter how she hated these people, she would show respect to them, for today anyway!

At the end of the party and very late in the evening, they were returned to Block 24 at Auschwitz One and converted back into their prison 'pyjamas' before the walk back to Auschwitz Birkenau.

Instantly a feeling of depression came over Margo. The beautiful princess had now turned back into a frog.

However, at least she smelled nice.

# CHAPTER 12
# OUT THROUGH THE IN DOOR

Over the next few months, nothing of any great note really happened in Peter's life. Margo had been sent to 'The Retreat' a further five times to waitress for the guards, so now Peter didn't worry anymore when she disappeared for a day or so.

The seasonal weather was now returning to cold and the Russian Army coat was once again a permanent fixture in Peter's wardrobe. He would be very grateful for this in a few weeks from now.

Talking about the Russian Army, he'd overheard the guards, his housemates in Kanada, talking of rumours that they were fast approaching in vast numbers and would very soon be amongst them.

For the most part, this scared the shit out of them, especially as when being guards at Auschwitz they hadn't seen any action for in some cases, three or four years. In fact, some of these guards had never seen any action at all and had never fired their guns in anger, only using them for target practise in the camp to scare the prisoners.

There was now a weird atmosphere about the place in general. All the guards had a suspicion that Germany was now losing the war, although those in the hierarchy would neither confirm nor deny this.

Even though the war might be almost over, the transport trains still arrived with increasing regularity. It was as though Herr Adolph himself wanted to be certain that as many Jews died before the enemy could deny him the chance of wiping them all off the face of the earth.

Peter had seen some wicked things during the past fifteen months, but one night he witnessed the worst atrocity of his stay at Auschwitz Birkenau when he was with William and Claus waiting for all the new arrivals to leave the cattle truck so they could begin the hunt for dead bodies and retrieve the luggage.

Josef Mengele no longer attended the selection party and left all decisions now to Heinz Kappler, who as noted before, sent mostly all the poor souls to the right and so to their appointment with the 'Cyclone 'B' gas.'

This one night, Peter watched in horror as a young family all jumped down together from the truck. In the commotion, the mother let go of their little boy's hand and he walked straight towards one of the dogs. The poor thing must have had a pet dog at home, as he showed no fear and must have thought it would be friendly.

The guard in charge of the animal made no attempt to pull the dog back, and as the child came closer, the dog set about him. Immediately, the dog had the poor boy's face in its mouth. It was literally ripping the child to pieces, as though it was playing with a rag doll.

The boy's parents were going wild, pleading with the guards to get the dog off their son, but all they did was laugh. The more the parents pleaded for the life of their little boy, the more raucous the laughter became.

Peter couldn't believe this. Surely many of these guards and officers had children of their own back home in Germany, so how could they be so callous towards another innocent child? How would Kappler have felt if that was his own children, Adolph or Eva, being ripped apart by this dog?

When seeing this vicious act, and not for the first time since he'd been incarcerated here, Peter's heart was breaking.

Christmas 1944 - Rudolph Höss cancelled the day of celebration this year, as he'd received orders from way on high that no guard should rest. There would now be no days off for the guards or officers, and especially the prisoners. Because of this, Margo and Peter could no longer spend Sundays in each other's company, so had to make do with their time together in the sorting room.

The good thing about this was that the 'nice lady guard' was now turning a blind eye to their antics and letting them spend a few moments each day together in the side room, the room where she'd taken Peter that time. It was good to be able to hold each other.

To make Margo feel better, Peter planned a marvellous future for the happy couple. They had a big house in the country, where the two of them would live with their five children, three girls and two boys.

"Oh Peter, will it happen?" she would ask, with hope in her heart.

"Of course it will, my darling," he'd reply. "I will make it happen for you. I promise."

We had now reached the third week of January 1945. This would be the beginning of the end for Auschwitz.

The entire camp was now in a state of panic. The Germans had had it confirmed that the Russian Army had reached Krakow, so were now less than thirty miles from Auschwitz Birkenau. This meant they were only a matter of days away from the camp. This should have made Peter happy, but it had completely the reverse effect.

"What are they going to do with all the prisoners left in here?" Peter asked a few of the Kanada Kommando, but without receiving an answer.

Even though he really wanted, and needed information, he didn't dare ask a Sonderkommando, and God forbid he questioned a Nazi guard!

He'd heard a few rumours and decided that he needed to discover the truth, so that night after work he would go and check for himself to see if one particular rumour was true. Sadly, that night, he discovered that it was.

Leaving the safety of Kanada, he rushed as fast as he could to Hut 44, but when he arrived, to his utter horror, the place was empty. He went in search of William Straus and when he found him, he questioned his friend.

"William, what happened to the Gypsies?" he queried.

"They were taken yesterday," William revealed. "Sorry, I thought you knew."

"Hell," Peter exasperated. "I didn't know. It could be us next."

"No Peter, haven't you heard?"

"Heard what?"

"Have you not heard the noise of them destroying the gas chambers?" William enquired.

"Why are they doing that?" Peter replied, answering with a question.

"I can only think they are expecting the Russians to arrive anytime soon and don't want to leave any evidence behind of what this place really was," William explained, but suggested it was only his theory.

"So do you think we are safe?" Peter asked. "Have we really survived?"

"Sadly not my friend, I think there is a good chance they will shoot us all," William stated. "Anyway, I think a bullet would be much quicker and less painful than fifteen minutes struggling for air and being gassed to death!"

"I don't want either," Peter quietly confessed. "And I really don't want Margo to die."

"Peter have you not noticed there are no longer any Sonderkommando in the camp?" Claus questioned the youngster.

"No not really. Why what happened?" Peter queried. His question was answered by William.

"Do you remember when you first came to Kanada when I told you about the Sonderkommando?" he began. "Well what I predicted, actually happened two days ago. They put a train load of arrivals into the gas chamber as normal, but this time, when the screaming stopped and they went inside to retrieve the bodies, the heavy metal gates were slammed closed behind them and the gas was thrown in from above. I'm telling you Peter, the big clean up has commenced."

Peter's worst nightmare began two days later. He entered the Kanada Sorting Room 10 to find it empty.

"MARGO!" he shouted as loud as his vocal chords would allow, but to no avail. There was no response!

Now in a mad state of panic, he rushed around like a headless chicken. He felt foolish for not knowing which room she'd been living in for all this time, but why would he? He would have been shot if found in the women's quarter of the building.

The entire place was empty, even the guards' room had been cleared. Where was she? Where was his Margo?

Running around the camp now, the only people he could still see were the very sick and feeble prisoners who'd been left to die. The SS figured they only had a few hours, a day at most to live, so why waste ammunition on these people.

Looking up, he noticed that even the watch towers were now empty. They contained no marksmen inside, and no machine guns were now being pointed at him. This place really was deserted!

He then heard voices in the distance and ran towards them. He reached the exit gate of Auschwitz Birkenau just in time to see all the girls from Kanada, about one hundred of them, being marched out of the camp on foot, accompanied by around twenty prison guards. He was horrified when he noticed the man leading them was Heinz Kappler. Knowing the fate of Margo was in Kappler's hands gave him a sinking feeling in the pit of his stomach!

"Margo – Margo – Margo," he kept shouting over, and over again until his throat was hoarse, but none of the girls showed any recognition of his voice, and no one turned around to face him.

"Margo – I love you," he kept shouting, until his lungs were almost at bursting point. Still nobody turned.

He had no idea if he'd been heard or not, but he hoped with all his heart that at least one person had heard him – his beautiful Margo.

"What are you doing here?" he heard a voice demand. He turned to face a lone gunman. "Why are you not going to the train?"

Peter suddenly realised that whilst he'd been searching for his loved one, the rest of Kanada, all the men from the Kanada Kommando had been rounded up and marched to the train siding.

He was marched there alone under gunpoint and soon found himself once again in the same cattle truck that he, William and Claus had cleared a thousand times before. He looked around for his two friends but couldn't see them, although he surmised they must be here on the train somewhere.

They were being transported, but to where, no one knew. However, the biggest question on Peter's mind was, whatever the destination, will they arrive?

He made his mind up there and then that no matter what happened on this journey, he was NOT going to die today. He was determined more than ever that he would survive. He had to, for his wonderful Margo.

He also remembered that he'd made a promise that one day he would kill Heinz Kappler, 'The Murderer of Auschwitz,' and to do this, he had to live.

No, Peter Florea was not going to die this day. This was something that he would not allow!

# CHAPTER 13
# THE GREAT ESCAPE

The train stopped and everyone was ordered to get off. "Alle raus! Schnell – Schnell," an SS guard was heard to shout.

Why were they stopping in the middle of nowhere? Peter was suspicious and decided to go ahead with his escape plan. He had no desire to die this day and had nothing to lose.

Waiting for the last prisoner to leave the cattle truck, he hung behind and glanced through a small hole in the wooden wall of the cattle truck. He noticed the guards were all busily rounding up the prisoners, for what, he didn't know, but this was his only chance to escape.

Taking one final glance at the guards and deciding that this was the time, he jumped down to the ground below and remained in a crouched position. He then did a backward flip, rolling under the carriage and between the wheels. As he rolled onto the rails the pain felt in his back was excruciating, but the adrenalin pumping through his body kept him going.

He waited a second or two and when he was sure that no one had seen him, he rolled completely to the other side of the tracks, where he stood up and under cover of the train; he began to run for his life!

The snow was fresh and deep, making it heavy going to get away, but get away he must. Without looking back, he ran as fast as his heavy legs would take him.

When he'd reached what he thought was around one hundred yards from the train, he heard gun fire, soon realising that he was the target. He could practically feel the wind of the bullets as they whizzed past, but not feeling any pain, he was convinced that he had not been hit.

Back at the train, the guards had stopped firing, not wishing to waste their bullets on just one prisoner when they had a hundred or more to slaughter!

"Go after him," the SS officer ordered to one of the younger guards.

"Shall I bring him back, Sir?" the younger man questioned.

"Why do that," the older man queried. "Does it matter where he dies? Shoot him where he stands." Obeying orders, the young guard took off in chase of the escapee.

Peter was by now becoming exhausted, however, even though he was at least two hundred yards ahead of his chaser, he could not afford to slow down, but then disaster struck!

He was only a few yards from the dense forest, but as he ran in the deep snow, it suddenly gave way and he fell into an even deeper hole! He tried to stand but it was obvious that he'd twisted his ankle and was clearly unable to go anywhere.

Resigned to the fact that he was about to die, he just sat down and waited, spending the last few seconds of his life thinking about what life could have been like for him and Margo.

He heard the crisp sound of jackboots cracking on the fresh snow as they approached. A few seconds later, he looked up to see the man who would finally end his life. He could not believe it when he saw it was Paul Fuster. They both looked at each other, each shocked to see the other.

"I am so sorry, Peter," Fuster said with sincerity.

Peter tried to smile, offering a bizarre kind of permission for the young man to administer the bullet.

Paul Fuster pulled his gun from the holster and pointed it at Peter's head. He delayed a few seconds but then moved his arm a couple of inches to his left and fired twice into the ground, easily missing his intended target by a couple of feet.

111

"Good luck, Peter," Fuster whispered to a stunned Peter, before replacing the gun in its holster and turning to walk away.

As Peter remained in the hole, he suddenly heard a rasp of machine gun fire followed by the sound of screaming. Slowly the screaming became quieter, until eventually stopping completely.

Instantly he thought of his beloved Margo. Had the same fate been dealt to her, was his darling girl now lying dead somewhere in a forest? He was very sad to be having these thoughts.

After a further ten minutes, he afforded himself a quick glance above the side of the ditch, just in time to see the cattle train pulling away in the same direction it had been heading when they'd stopped. It was obvious to Peter that he was the only survivor. Everyone else, including William and Claus had been mercilessly slaughtered! Paul Fuster had not only spared his life, he'd saved it.

A feeling of euphoria spread through his body, giving him the strength to crawl his way the extra few yards to reach the relative cover of the forest.

After waiting for as long as he could stand the cold, under cover of darkness and the foliage of the trees, he made his way through the forest to find somewhere warmer to sleep for the night. Although his ankle was still painful, the threat of his being frozen to death on this bitterly cold Polish January night was more than enough incentive to block the pain from his mind and persevere with the journey.

He eventually came to a clearing and could make out the silhouette of what looked like a small farmhouse in the distance. With renewed energy, he made his way to the building to see if it could possibly be his resting place for the night. He was so tired he could have slept anywhere, but it had to be a place of safety.

Looking around, as he got closer he could see that this must have once been a working farm, but no doubt the German Army had commandeered the livestock, probably to feed their troops. He felt sorry for the family who lived here, but this was a problem for tomorrow. Tonight he must sleep.

He found his way to what must once have been the cowshed and thought it could be a good place to rest. He then thought of the irony of this situation. He'd just escaped death by running away from a cattle truck, and now here he was, seeking sanctuary in a cowshed!

He discovered a wooden ladder taking him to the upper tier of the shed and found bundles of unused hay lying there. Thinking it would be a good place to hide as well as to sleep; he curled up on his hay mattress and was soon sleeping soundly.

# CHAPTER 14
# HOT VEGETABLE SOUP

Peter woke abruptly when he felt a sharp pain in his left thigh. He looked up to see an older man standing over him holding a pitchfork and ready to attack.

"Who are you boy, and what are you doing here?" the older man demanded.

"I'm sorry, Sir, I do not mean to cause any problems for you," Peter began. "Being tired and cold last night, I needed somewhere warm and dry to sleep. I never intended to cause you any offence."

Seeing the young boy was no danger to him, he removed the threat of the pitchfork from Peter's leg.

"Where are you from boy?" he demanded.

"I come from Budapest," Peter replied.

"What? Budapest in Hungary?" the man asked incredulously.

"Yes Sir," Peter confirmed.

"Boy, you are a long way from home," the man observed. "And why are you dressed in those strange clothes, especially that Russian Army coat?"

"I ran away from the train transporting the prisoners to their deaths," Peter revealed, worried now that this man might be a Jew hater and would hand him back to the enemy.

"The train transporting the prisoners to their deaths?" the man repeated. "What on earth are you talking about?"

Peter began telling the man about his story, but when he reached the point about Auschwitz Birkenau and how it was a death camp, the older man suggested they go to the farmhouse and get comfortable, and then Peter could continue with his story.

Entering the farmhouse, Peter found himself confronted by a rather rotund looking woman, the likes of which he hadn't seen for a very long time. She didn't know whether to smile or not as he entered, but chose to smile anyway.

"What is your name, boy?" the man asked.

"My name is Peter, Sir, Peter Florea," the young lad returned.

"My name is Rubin and this is my wife, Stephanie," the man said, introducing the woman. "But everyone calls her Steph, so I suggest you do the same."

"Thank you," Peter replied, not really knowing what else to say.

"I expect you are hungry," the woman said. "I have a nice pot of soup in the stockpot."

'Soup,' Peter thought, 'I've been eating nothing but soup for almost one and a half years!' This is what he thought, but what he did say was, "That sounds wonderful. Thank you very much."

"Here you go," Steph announced, presenting him with the soup, but not in a big tin mug but a lovely china bowl.

He had to admit it looked nothing like the swill he'd been eating in Auschwitz. This soup was full of potato, leeks and carrots, with onions and lentils. To Peter, it looked like Heaven in a bowl. To top it off, Steph presented it to him with a lovely big chunk of homemade bread. "Baked fresh this morning," she smiled.

The couple watched as the young man devoured the food placed before him, realising that the poor soul was actually starving.

"Would you like some more?" Steph asked, as he wiped the bowl clean with his bread.

"No," Rubin said sternly. "It could be dangerous for his stomach to overeat after being starved for so long."

Steph agreed, even though being a mother, it was her natural instinct to also be a feeder.

"You can have some more a little later, Peter," she told him. "Now tell us all about that camp you've been staying in."

Steph and Rubin listened to his story, gripped, as Peter told them about the past sixteen months of his life. They were shocked when they heard about the gas chambers and crematoria, the constant putrid smell and how the black smoke bellowed out through the chimneys for twenty-four hours, each, and every day.

Steph was clearly moved when hearing about his love for Margo, and when he told her that he didn't know if she was now dead or alive, she couldn't help herself. She jumped up from her seat and rushed to comfort the lad, flinging her arms around him and squeezing him tightly.

Peter then did something he'd not done in all the time since leaving Budapest and being in the hell of Auschwitz Birkenau – He cried like a baby!

"Oh Peter, you poor boy," Steph declared, beginning to bawl herself. She couldn't believe how all this could have been happening under their noses in their own country, with nobody even hearing about it.

"How old are you, son?" Rubin questioned.

"I'm not really sure," Peter admitted and then questioned. "What date is it?"

"It's the twenty-sixth of January," Steph confirmed.

"But what year is it?" the confused lad questioned.

"Good lord, it's nineteen forty-five," Steph informed the youngster.

"In that case, I am seventeen years and eight months old," Peter replied. "I will be eighteen in May – May the twenty-third."

116

"My God," Rubin exclaimed. "How can all these things happen to someone so young? I feel ashamed that we did not do something about this."

"But Rubin," Peter began, "there is nothing that you or anyone else could have done for the people in that camp. But you are doing something now."

"What?" Rubin queried.

"You are helping me and I am thankful for it," Peter revealed.

The couple said nothing, but once again, Steph threw her arms around Peter and held him even tighter. As she did this, Peter closed his eyes and imagined it was Margo hugging him, and in his imagination, for a brief moment – it was.

"Okay, we need to get organised," Rubin declared, suddenly appearing to snap into action. "We need to burn those prison clothes and that Russian Army coat, because if anyone sees you wearing that around here, you will surely be shot on sight."

"But what will I wear?" Peter questioned, almost pleading.

"You can wear our son's clothes," Steph told the lad. "He would be about your size, or at least he was the last time we saw him."

"You have a son?" Peter queried. "What happened to him?" As soon as he asked this question, he feared the worst.

"He joined the Polish Resistance," Rubin said. "We haven't seen, or heard from him for nearly a year now. We have no idea if he's dead or alive, but we are still hopeful and also both very proud of him."

"You should be proud," Peter stated. "If he is still alive, I hope he finds Heinz Kappler and kills the murdering bastard!"

Steph smiled at the lad. "Let's hope so," she agreed and then continued. "Now, how would you like a little more of that soup? You need fattening up, boy."

"Thank you," Peter smiled. "But how about me having a lot more of that soup and getting really fat?" he laughed, joined by both Steph and her husband, Rubin.

Peter was so grateful that he'd ended up in this place with these wonderful people. He knew that being here he was in safe hands and even better company.


A little later, dressed as a young man again in normal clothes and with a full belly, the youngster sat in front of the roaring log fire in the centre of the room. His eyes began to get heavy, and with all the recent excitement, he was soon sleeping soundly.

When he woke, he saw Rubin in the garden with another roaring fire, but this one was burning his prison clothes, including the Russian Army coat. He went outside to see the final death of those 'pyjamas' and the realization suddenly hit him that, at last, he was no longer a prisoner of Auschwitz and Heinz Kappler held no fear for him any longer.

The two men stood in silence for a few minutes watching the smoke spiral through the air. To Peter, it felt like a funeral service, where he was mourning the death of many thousands of people during the past months of his life. He still could not believe that he'd survived Auschwitz Birkenau, when not many of the other prisoners had.

Rubin looked at the young man and it was as though he could see what he was thinking. Peter returned the look and the older man gave him a smile.

Looking at Rubin now, he couldn't help but smile. Unlike his wife Steph, where she was plump, Rubin was very thin, although he was not Auschwitz Birkenau thin. Where those poor souls were walking bags of skin and bones, Rubin was a 'normal' thin, if there was such a description.

He had hair to the sides of his head but nothing on top, being completely bald on the scalp. In contrast, he had a big bushy beard, which Peter thought must have taken years to grow, but was obviously well taken care of. The youngster smiled when he thought to himself that Rubin had an 'upside down' head!

Even though the temperature was cold, the older man seemed to have an all year round brownness to his face and arms, probably caused from working constantly outdoors on the land and in the sun.

"What are your plans, Peter?" Rubin asked the youngster.

"I suppose eventually I want to return home to my family in Budapest," he revealed. "But first I need to get to Warsaw."

"Warsaw," Rubin said. "Why do you want to go to Warsaw?"

"I heard the guards at Auschwitz Birkenau mention that the records kept in the camp will be sent there after the war. The one thing with the Nazis is that they did keep meticulous records of all the people who came through the gates of the camp." He stopped and showed Rubin his prison tattoo. "I was number Two-Nine-Eight-Six-One," he explained.

"Good God! What is wrong with those people?" was all Rubin could offer.

"I'll leave in a day or two, but will take a rest first," Peter said, declaring his future intentions.

"What do you mean, son," Rubin remarked. "You cannot leave now. They will capture you."

"But surely the war is over now," Peter observed.

"Peter, the war is not over," Rubin gently informed the lad. "It's true the Russians are pushing the German army back, but they are still occupying most of Poland. You want to go to Warsaw?"

"Yes."

"Well you cannot, because Warsaw is still very much in the hands of the Nazis and will be for a good few months yet."

Rubin looked at the youngster and could see the sadness in his face, so added, "But you are welcome to stay here for as long as is needed. You are welcome to stay here with Steph and me."

"Thank you," Peter replied. Although he was sad to hear this information, he was also happy and grateful to be staying on the farm with these wonderful people.

A couple of weeks later, Peter was toiling in the field when he spotted three men on the horizon. He went to the house to alert Rubin and the elder man went outside to meet them. Peter went to stand by the side of his friend, but then realised they were being approached by three German soldiers.

"Let me do the talking, Peter," Rubin ordered.

As they reached the two, they could see that the three soldiers looked totally worn out and drained of any energy. Rubin didn't speak; he waited for them to say what they needed to say.

"Please," one said politely, "do you have any food you can give us?"

"We only have soup prepared, but you are welcome to have some," Rubin informed the men. "You are welcome to come inside but you must leave your rifles out here. I will not have guns inside the house."

"But we cannot do that," one soldier pleaded.

"If you do not leave your guns outside, you will not be welcome in my house," Rubin told them again.

"But we could just shoot you and take all your food AND your house," said another of the German soldiers.

"But you won't do that," Rubin said sternly. "Look lads, for that's what you are, young lads, I can see you are involved in a war you don't want to be in. I can see you are good men and you are welcome inside my home – but the guns are not. You have to leave your guns outside," he repeated again.

Hearing Rubin say this again, all three men conceded defeat, lay down their weapons and went inside to where Steph was waiting.

"Come on in, come inside and you get yourselves warm, boys," she instructed. Yes, these young men were Germans, but Steph did not have an ounce of malice in her body.

Peter looked at Rubin and his wife with a new found admiration. Rubin was such a brave man to refuse three armed soldiers entrance to his property, whilst Steph was such a lovely woman to feed these Germans, of whom her country had suffered invasion.

He then took a closer look at the three, noting they looked absolutely done in! Peter couldn't believe these young men were part of the same war machine that had provided the soldiers to guard the prisoners and run the Auschwitz Birkenau death camp.

As they sat at the table eating Steph's wonderful homemade soup, they told their story. They'd been marching through the undergrowth when their company came under attack by an advancing party of Russians. Being ambushed, and taken by total surprise, most of their brothers in arms were slaughtered.

They'd managed to get away in the heat of battle and had basically run away as fast as they could, an action which would bring them the firing squad, should they be caught as deserters.

"And you, what's your story?" one of the soldiers asked of Peter.

"Don't worry about Peter," Rubin interrupted. "He's only a seventeen year old boy. He is not your enemy. He's no danger to you."

121

The three all seemed to accept this and no more was spoken on the subject.

"If you would like to stay for a while and rest for a few days," Rubin began, "you are welcome to sleep outside in the cowshed. It will be warm and dry for you in there."

Peter thought of the irony of this situation. The very place where he'd sought sanctuary not too many days ago was the same place where these men, the potential enemy, would also be hiding from the might of the German army.

In the end the German lads, Patrick, Werner and Christian ended up staying almost a week, but decided to leave the area in case more Russians came and found them hiding here.

Like Peter, they'd also grown a deep affection for Rubin and Steph and because of this, didn't want to get them into trouble. After all, if the advancing Russian Army came and found them in hiding here on the farm, they could maybe think that Rubin and Steph were collaborators and would have treated them badly, maybe even killing them.

The strangest thing about all this was that Peter and the three had also become rather friendly, which truly strengthened his argument that not all of the German race were bad people. Most were good, but following the orders of extremely bad and wicked people, especially a silly little man with a stupid moustache!

On the day they left, all six formed a huddle and hugged each other tightly and shaking hands with extreme vigour. Steph presented them with a large basket full of freshly baked bread.

"Fresh from the oven for the journey," she proclaimed.

"Good luck boys. I hope you can find and rejoin your army so they don't think you have deserted," Rubin said. "But please don't kill anyone if you can help it. You lads are far too good for that."

When they came to Peter, Werner said something that he would remember for the rest of his life.

"Peter, we are all so very sorry for everything you have gone through in your short life," he announced. "I hope you find your Margo, and I hope with all my heart that she is still alive and you will spend the rest of your life with her."

"Please forgive us," Christian pleaded.

"Be happy," Patrick smiled. "And if I find Heinz Kappler, I will do my best to kill him for you!"

Peter, Steph and Rubin watched the lads until they disappeared over the brow of the hill.

"Nice lads," Steph said eventually, with just the merest hint of a tear in her eye.

"Yes, it was a pleasure to have them stay with us," Rubin agreed.

"And they never did bring their rifles inside the house," Peter joked. As he said this, all three of them began laughing.

"More vegetable soup, Peter?" asked Steph with a smile.

"Yes please," Peter grinned.

"Then more vegetable soup it is," Rubin added.

# CHAPTER 15
# LIBERATION

A few weeks after the young Germans had left the farm; life for Peter was slowly getting back to some kind of normality. There was a rumour that all enemy troops had left the area after being chased away by the Red Army, or fleeing, in case they encountered the foe.

They knew all was lost and they knew they were losing the fight, so what was the point of dying at this late stage of the war?

Because of this, Rubin was a lot more relaxed these days and had a surprise for Peter.

"Shall I fetch it, Steph?" he asked his wife.

"Yes," she replied. "Go and dig it up."

"I hope it still works," Rubin said hopefully.

"What are you talking about?" Peter asked with curiosity.

"You'll see," Steph informed the lad. "Don't be so impatient."

"The impatience of youth," Rubin laughed. "Come with me, Peter. You can help with the digging."

A by now very curious Peter followed Rubin. They left the house and walked towards a large wooden building which was about the same size as the cowshed, but which the youngster had never been inside before.

"What is this place?" asked an inquisitive Peter.

"This is where we stored the hay for the animal feed when we had cattle, before the Germans took them all," Rubin told him. "They looked in here briefly, but thank the lord they didn't take a more thorough search."

As he entered the wooden structure, Peter could see bales of hay stacked floor to ceiling. Rubin went to the corner of the room and began moving the bales around.

"Here we are, son," he announced. "Come here and start digging."

Peter did as instructed and around two feet down, he hit something solid.

"Careful Peter," Rubin shouted," be gentle. Don't break it."

"Don't break what?" Peter questioned, still curious.

"You'll see," Rubin remarked, smiling.

The young man looked down at the hole in the ground and spotted something that looked like a wooden box, with hay wrapped around to keep it safe.

"It's a wooden box!" he claimed, a little sarcastically.

"No it's not," Rubin laughed. "Here, I'll give you a hand to get it out."

The two of them made much lighter work of lifting the object from the ground than Peter would have done alone. As they lifted it out a little further, Peter was able to take a closer look at the object.

"It's a radio!" he shouted, excited by the discovery. "But why is it buried out here?"

"When they first invaded Poland, the Nazis told everyone to hand in any radios they may have in their homes. They gave them so many days to do this, and after that, anyone caught with a radio would have it confiscated and they would receive punishment, normally a beating. If you were caught actually listening to the radio, they would smash it to pieces in front of you, and then take you outside and shoot you and all your family."

"So you took one hell of a risk?" Peter claimed, with more than a hint of admiration.

"No not really," Rubin instructed. "If they'd found it, they would have only given me a beating. But Peter, you have seen where it was buried, do you really think there was any chance it would be found?"

"You are a very clever man," Peter smiled. This comment was answered with a huge but playful slap on the youngster's back!

"Peter, this is not the only thing hidden in this building," Rubin confessed.

"What else is there?" the youngster questioned his older friend.

"Take a look at this," the older man ordered.

"What? I don't see anything," Peter stated.

"Patience son," Rubin told the lad. "Give me a hand, but only take out a couple of bales as we need to keep this hidden from everyone, including the locals."

By now, Peter was extremely excited to see what the removal of hay might reveal, and so he went to work. With Rubin's help, he moved about fifteen bales away from the side of a huge pile. He then noticed a sheet of shiny black metal.

"Is that what I think it is?" the youngster queried.

"If you think it's a car, then you would be correct," Rubin admitted.

The two hurriedly went to work removing a few more bales to reveal a 'Polski Fiat Mazur 518,' which Rubin and Steph had bought brand new in 1935.

"How did the Germans' miss this?" Peter asked.

"They were not looking for cars, only food," Rubin smiled.

"Does it work?" Peter questioned.

"I don't know about that, but it will after I play around with it," Rubin stated. "It must be ten years old now but has not been driven since the beginning of the war," he said, smiling at

Peter, who by now was hanging on to his every word. "However, when we heard of the invasion, before I hid the car I made sure it had a full tank of petrol in the tank."

"You are such a wise man," Peter beamed.

After finally covering the car back up again and retrieving the full mass of the radio, the two carried it to the house. Peter could see why Rubin asked for help. With the many valves inside it was heavy as hell! It was all worth it however, once it was connected to the power supply and switched on.

An air of expectancy awaited the two, as the valves took a minute or two to warm. A few seconds later, the pair punched the air as music suddenly began streaming through the speaker. Steph looked at the two men and suddenly noticed that Peter had tears in his eyes.

"My dear boy, why are you crying?" she questioned him.

"Sorry," he said.

"Don't be silly, Peter," Steph stressed. "What's the matter? Why are you so emotional?"

"Sorry," Peter repeated. "It's just that the last time I heard music playing, I was with Margo listening to the camp orchestra performing in the main square."

There was nothing Steph could say about this, and so instead, she threw her arms around Peter and offered him comfort whilst he wept. She found it painful how much he loved Margo, the wonderful girl he'd lost.

"We'll be able to listen to the news from London every evening now, Peter," Rubin said, trying to comfort the lad. "The BBC news readers will tell us the truth."

"The BBC, what's that?" Peter questioned.

"Sorry Peter – The British Broadcasting Corporation, based in London, England," Rubin informed the youngster.

"Come on Peter," Steph said, trying her best to cheer up the young man. "Come and dance with me." He tried to resist but she was having none of it and pulled him from the seat. "Come on Peter – dance."

The two began moving to the beat and frolicking in time to the music. Peter couldn't help but laugh when he noticed Steph's stomach flab wobbling in a different direction to the rest of her. At least for a few moments his memories were removed from the events of the past sixteen months, his beautiful Margo, and the hellhole that was Auschwitz Birkenau.

Every night, the three of them sat together religiously to listen to the news being broadcast from London. They were excited to hear of the American, Canadian and British Army's progress through France and Belgium.

"It's only a matter of time now, Peter," Rubin announced. "They'll be in Berlin soon and that little moustached bastard will be forced to surrender."

"I hope they hang the bastard!" Peter said surprising Steph, who'd never heard the lad blaspheme too many times before. However, she could understand the reason why, so didn't chastise him.

One evening, they were settling down to listen to the news as normal, when a very emotional man came on the radio to broadcast to the world. The story he told was something quite unbelievable.

"I have just returned from the Belsen Concentration Camp. I find it very hard and heartbreaking to describe the scenes I have witnessed," he began.

The man then went on to describe how the British Army had liberated a concentration camp at Bergen-Belsen on the 15th of April 1945. They'd found thousands of dead bodies, not much more than rotting corpses, which they made the captured SS officers bury, whilst survivors who were fit enough looked on, taunting and swearing at these people who only days earlier had been their tormentors!

The SS officers were made to bury seventeen thousand bodies before being taken away to face a trial. There were still at least eight thousand dead victims left to bury, which the British lads would do. The announcer said that he thought these young boys would be scarred and have nightmares about this for the rest of their lives.

He described the smell as being terrible, like nothing he'd ever smelled before, or was likely to smell again in the future. He said that many of the survivors were riddled with lice, which he witnessed climbing the walls of the huts where the people were caged. Many were suffering with typhus, the biggest killer in the camp. They were also suffering from extreme hunger and were like walking skeletons, many not even having the strength to leave the huts.

As the broadcaster continued, Peter and Rubin both looked at Steph and could see she was now gently sobbing in the corner of the room. It was now Peter's turn to comfort her, as she'd done for him now, many times.

"Oh Peter. Was this what it was like where you were?" she asked through her tears.

"Not really," Peter confessed. "Most people died within an hour of arriving at Auschwitz Birkenau, so only suffered for fifteen minutes or so. The rest of us suffered in different ways, being worked, sometimes to death, and beaten when we couldn't work.

It was only in the last few weeks I was there when we saw people dying from disease or hunger and being left where they fell. Before this, they were always taken to the crematorium after passing away. I think if anything, these poor lost souls in Bergen Belsen had it far worse than we did in Auschwitz Birkenau. God bless them."

"Come on you two. Cheer up," Rubin ordered, attempting to lighten the mood whilst studying his map. "You know what this means?"

"No Rubin, what does it mean?" Steph queried.

"The British Army has liberated the camp at Bergen Belsen. This means they are only one hundred and eighty miles from Berlin. It can only be a number of days now, a week or two at the most, especially with the Russians in hot pursuit from the other direction. The war will soon be over." This revelation certainly put a smile on everyone's face.

Rubin's assumptions were proved to be correct when twenty-three days later, on the 8th of May 1945, the three gathered together to listen to the BBC broadcast and there was another announcement. This time it was the Prime Minister, Winston Churchill, who was to address the nation.

"What's this?" Rubin asked curiously, as Churchill began to speak.

"Yesterday, at two forty-one in the morning," he began, "a representative of the German high command signed an unconditional surrender of all German land, sea and air in Europe. The war is over. We have victory in Europe."

The three could only stare at each other, not really knowing what to do or say. Then, simultaneously they all leapt into the air and began screaming! The war was over. The end of almost six years of hell had finally come to a close.

After all this elation, Peter suddenly began feeling strange. He was celebrating the end of the war whilst at the same time mourning the loss of Margo. His elation turned to a feeling of despair, as he wondered what he was supposed to do now.

There was only one thing for it. No matter the outcome, he had to discover what happened to his beloved girl. Whether dead or alive, he had to find out what had happened to his beautiful, Margo Koval.

For today though, it was celebration day. Steph insisted on more dancing and they partied well into the night.

This was a day he would never forget for the remainder of his life, the 8$^{th}$ of May 1945 – Victory in Europe Day.

# CHAPTER 16
# THE SMILING ASSASSIN

Although the war in Europe was now officially over, Peter still had some torrid nightmares where he would wake in a cold sweat, convinced he was still a prisoner and back in captivity at Auschwitz Birkenau. The good thing about having these scary dreams was that every night, he was reunited with his darling Margo.

At the beginning of the war, Rubin, being the very clever man he was, had buried money in the hay barn close to where he'd entombed the radio. It was not a fortune, but it was enough to buy some cows and a bull to service them. From this, he hoped to develop a herd over the next few years. Although he knew it would be a slow process, he had to start somewhere.

He'd also bought some hens, so every morning they had fresh eggs and milk for breakfast. To Peter, after his meagre offerings in the camp, this was a little touch of heaven!

All three had discussed Peter's future. He wanted to go to the capital city of Warsaw to see if they had any records of survivors from the camps. Until he knew for certain what had been Margo's fate, he had to keep searching for her.

However, it was decided that even though the war had ended, there could still be small pockets of soldiers meandering about who might like to take pot-shots at anyone they found along the way. Maybe, as Hitler had done at the end of the First World War, they didn't agree with the surrender!

Although there was no proof of this, it was Steph's theory. Therefore, to keep her happy, Peter told her he would wait until news came through about the safety of travelling.

Young Peter was toiling in the field one afternoon, planting potatoes, carrots and cabbages, when he heard Steph let out a scream from the house. He immediately downed tools and ran to her aid. When he arrived inside the house, he found her with a stranger in the kitchen.

"Are you okay, Steph?" he demanded. "And who is this?"

He then noticed she was not scared, she was happy. In fact, she was very happy! In fact, Steph was ecstatic!

"Peter, this is our son," she said tearfully. "He has returned to us. He has survived the war."

The young man walked to Peter and shook his hand. "Hello Peter, I have heard all about you. My mother and father speak very highly of you, so you as far as I'm concerned, you are more than welcome here in my family home," he announced.

"Thank you," Peter replied.

"This is our son, Thomas," Steph offered.

"Tom, please," the young man pleaded.

"Very pleased to meet you, Tom," Peter smiled.

The two men sat together and had a chat about their wartime experiences, although Peter sensed that Rubin and Steph's offspring did not want to say too much or go into any great detail in front of his parents.

Tom had been a normal young man, not much older than a child when the Germans' came and stripped his parents of their livelihoods by stealing their cows and chickens. He'd become so incensed that day by those actions that he ran away to join the Polish Resistance and had been fighting the enemy ever since.

"Did you kill anyone?" Peter asked quietly.

"I don't really know, but I suppose I could have," Tom replied with honesty. "My job was damaging property used by the enemy. I dynamited rail tracks and bridges to stop the ammunition and provisions arriving at the front line, that type of thing. I was never involved in any face to face combat."

"It's a shame you didn't blow up the rail line which took the condemned to Auschwitz Birkenau," Peter said sadly.

"Yes, my father told me about your experiences at that awful place," Tom told Peter almost apologetically. "That must have been terrible for you."

"Not as bad for me as for some. At least I survived," Peter stressed.

"Mum told me about your girlfriend," Tom divulged.

"Yes," Peter answered. "My lovely Margo, Margo Koval."

"You have to try to find her, Peter," Tom offered.

"I think she's dead," Peter said sadly.

"But you don't know that for a fact," Tom claimed. "And until you know for certain, you cannot give up. You have to keep searching for her."

"I will," Peter said honestly, having every intention of looking for her until he knew for certain what had been her fate.

"If I can, I will help you," Tom offered.

"Thank you," Peter replied. "The first thing I must do when I can is get myself to Warsaw. I've heard that's where they keep the war records."

"But Peter," Tom said softly. "Warsaw has been destroyed! There are only a few thousand people still living there amongst the rubble." He looked in his direction and could see he looked forlorn. "I think that maybe we should look in Krakow," he said. Instantly he saw the smile return to Peter's face.

"Was Krakow damaged?" the youngster questioned.

"Not at all," Tom confirmed. He went on to tell Peter that unlike Warsaw, which had been bombed incessantly and practically destroyed by the Russian Air Force, they had left Krakow and most other places in Poland alone.

"I must get to Krakow then," Peter confirmed.

"We will go together," Tom offered.

"That would be really great," Peter smiled.


A few days later the two, now firm friends, were sitting outside in the field and enjoying the warmth of the May sunshine when Tom suddenly came over all melancholic.

"Are you feeling alright?" Peter questioned.

"I'm okay," Tom replied. "I am just thinking about a girl I knew in the resistance. It's funny because I haven't thought about her for a long time now."

"Was she your girlfriend?" Peter questioned.

"Not really, but I would have liked her to have been," Tom admitted.

"Maybe it's not too late. You should look for her," the younger of the two suggested.

"It wouldn't be any use," Tom revealed, "because she was executed by the Nazis. They put her in front of a firing squad and murdered her."

Peter gave Tom his complete attention as he went on to tell the story.

"Her name was Patricia Soloneski, but the Germans knew her as 'The Smiling Assassin," Tom began. "I met her a few weeks after joining the resistance, when on a bombing raid to blow up rail tracks just outside of Warsaw. I liked her immediately. She had the face of an angel, with beautiful blonde hair and deep blue eyes you felt you could dive into."

"That's exactly how I would have described my Margo," Peter butted in. "Must be a Polish trait." He then listened as Tom continued with his story about Patricia.

135

"With her slight frame she looked more like a schoolgirl than a member of the resistance, the type of girl men wanted to take care of and look after. She had the look of a young girl who needed to be protected, but in reality she could, and would kill in seconds, any Nazi who stood in her way."

Tom went on to tell Peter about the time when running the Warsaw Ghetto the Germans banned the Poles from using the cinema on Marschallstrasse. Patricia simply strolled into the Germans-only, 'Kammerlichtspiele' wearing a fake pregnancy suit in which she was hiding a bomb. She'd set the timer and managed to get in and plant it among the seated SS officers and get out just in time. It exploded whilst she was outside in the street, killing more than one hundred of the enemy.

She also managed to get inside a German only officers club dressed as a waitress. Before they realised what was going on, she'd killed six of them and left a further eight badly wounded. None of the survivors could describe what she looked like.

"However the bravest and most heroic thing Patricia ever did," Tom continued, "was when she casually walked inside the Gestapo Headquarters situated in the high security Police district of Warsaw. Her target was an SS officer named Franz Kaufmann.

A few weeks earlier, Kaufmann had had fifty Polish political prisoners publicly hanged and left on the gallows for more than a day to warn others to 'toe the line.' This naturally incensed Patricia and she took it upon herself to give recompense.

She walked into the Gestapo offices dressed as a farm girl, once again wearing the pregnancy suit. Asking to see Kaufmann, the two guards, thinking she was the officer's pregnant girlfriend, smiled at her and gave her a pass, and even gave directions to his office. Once inside the office, from below the pregnant disguise she produced a gun fitted with a silencer and shot Kaufmann in the head. She then calmly walked out, but not before killing the two guards at the entrance on the way."

"Wow! That's amazing," Peter offered.

"But the story didn't end there," Tom went on to say. "A couple of days later, it was discovered that Kaufmann had survived the attack and been taken to hospital. Patricia was really angry about this, particularly about the fact that she hadn't completed the mission properly."

"What did she do?" Peter questioned, now gripped by all this being revealed to him.

"She walked into the hospital dressed as a doctor in a white coat and a stethoscope around her neck, found Kaufmann's room and completed her task. She shot the SS officer dead, plus the two soldiers guarding him. After this, she casually dropped the coat and instrument on the floor and walked out dressed in civilian clothes."

Tom looked at Peter and could see he was very engrossed by the story.

"So what happened to her?" Peter questioned.

"Well, by now the Gestapo were so angry, and to a certain extent, scared about 'The Smiling Assassin' that they offered a reward for her capture, offering one hundred and fifty thousand zlotys for information leading to her arrest. Now this is where she'd made her only mistake, and it was a big one."

"What was this mistake," an exited Peter questioned. Tom stopped to take a sharp intake of breath before continuing.

"Because she'd been so successful and never been suspected of being anything but a sweet young girl, she still lived alone in her parents apartment.

One night when arriving home, the Gestapo were waiting for her. Although pleading her innocence, someone in the

137

apartment block had given her identity away and claimed the reward. This person was never discovered, and if they had been, they would also be dead by now!

Before being taken away by her captors, Patricia tried to take a cyanide pill but was stopped. They wanted her to be taken alive."

Tom stopped for a moment to wipe the tears from his eyes. He was getting very emotional now.

"What happened to Patricia?" Peter queried, although in his heart, he already knew the end of the story.

"We didn't know for sure what happened until the end of the war. I have met other resistance members who were in the Gestapo prison at the same time as Patricia. They told me she was interrogated and tortured for many weeks, but had never revealed any names, places or secrets to her interrogators.

Eventually these captors gave up, knowing she would never tell them anything about the movement, and so she was executed, quietly, and with no pomp or ceremony. The Gestapo thought that to do so would only glorify her part in terrorising them."

"What a woman," Peter stated. "You must be very proud to have known her."

"Yes I am," Tom admitted. "But she was not a woman - she was never allowed to be a woman. She was only eighteen years of age when executed."

"I'm very sorry for your loss," Peter offered.

"Thank you, Peter, but at least I know my love can never be," Tom said. "You on the other hand are still in limbo. You don't know if your Margo is alive or not."

"Yes that is correct, I don't," Peter admitted sadly.

So let's go and look for her!" Tom announced.

# CHAPTER 17
# KRAKOW

The car was motoring beautifully. Even though it had not been driven for at least six years, after Rubin had cleaned the plugs and points and given the engine a little tweak, it was now running smoothly. That was after Peter and Tom had given it a push for Rubin to jumpstart the engine because of the flat, unused battery, which now the car was running, was holding charge.

"Good car, this," Rubin smiled as they left the farm to begin the journey to Krakow.

Once he'd heard the lads' plans, Rubin insisted on driving them to the city. Steph, although supporting the decision, was adamant on staying home alone to look after the farm. Tom had offered to stay with her, but she told him in no uncertain terms that his help would be of better use helping Peter with his dream of finding 'his' Margo.

It was now mid September. Daytime temperatures were pleasantly warm, but with cooler evenings. The war in Europe was by now well and truly over, although they listened to the radio each night to hear the news of the fighting still going on with the Japanese on the other side of the world.

A few days earlier, Rubin called to Peter to come inside the house. He'd heard of news on the radio.

"Did you know of a Josef Kramer when you were in Auschwitz Birkenau, Peter?" he questioned the lad.

"I never knew him, but I knew of him. Some of my gypsy friends told me about him," Peter confirmed. "Apparently he made Heinz Kappler seem like a choirboy! He left the camp before I arrived – thank the lord. There was also a girl with him who was particularly vicious with the women prisoners."

"Irma Grese," Rubin offered.

"Yes, but how do you know?" Peter queried.

"It's just been on the radio," Rubin informed him. "Irma Grese travelled to be with Kramer at Bergen Belsen. She became the warden of the women's section there, whilst Josef Kramer was the camp commandant."

"I have heard stories about them when at Auschwitz," Peter began. "I was told by my gypsy friend, Oswald, of a rumour that she'd had an affair with Josef Mengele, the doctor known as the 'Beast of Auschwitz.' Because of this, she was allowed to select the women for the gas chamber, and it was rumoured that she only chose the prettiest ones so she had no competition for Mengele's affections.

My friend also told me stories of her raping other women prisoners in the camp and having many affairs with many different SS officers. Apparently, she also forced some of the Jewish male prisoners to have sex with her! Oswald said she was very nasty piece of work!"

As he told Rubin this, a shudder swept through his body as he thought about his time in the death camp. "Why do you ask?" he questioned Rubin.

"You remember back in April when we heard the news that the camp at Bergen Belsen had been liberated by the British?" Rubin stopped to wait for a reply, but when none came, he continued. "Well Josef Kramer and Irma Grese, along with forty-three other guards from Belsen have just gone on trial at a place called Luneburg. That's a town only a few miles from where the camp had been."

"Had been?" Peter queried.

"Yes. The British destroyed the camp a few days after the liberation. They burned all the huts there to kill any disease which may have been contained within them," Rubin confirmed.

An instant panic came into the mind of Peter as he realised that, as he'd not had the time to retrieve his stash of goodies from the side of Kanada because he hadn't had the time to do so during his last day at the camp, there was a possibility that Auschwitz Birkenau had also been destroyed, along with the rest of the structures.

Was it wrong of him to hope the Russian liberators had done no damage and left the camp intact? He panicked even more when realising that one day he would have to return to Auschwitz Birkenau in an attempt to collect his stash.

"Let's hope the bastards hang!" Tom said with real anger to his voice.

"I hope that bastard Kappler dies, swinging at the end of a rope," Peter announced. "And I hope I am there to witness it. I want to look into his eyes when he takes his last breath. I want him to see me smiling."

This was a side to Peter that Rubin hadn't ever truly seen before. Although he didn't really like seeing the youngster like this, he could understand the reason for his anger and hatred.

As they motored along through the country lanes of southern Poland, they passed little cottages by the roadside, many with people sitting outside and waving to them as they passed. Peter noticed they were all still painfully thin, although not 'camp thin.'

Even though the war had been over for quite a few weeks by now, food was still in desperately short supply. Peter realised how lucky he'd been to be living on the farm with Rubin, Steph, and now Tom. For him, that morning when he'd woken with the pitchfork rammed into his leg was the last day he'd been hungry, although being in the Kanada Kommando at Auschwitz Birkenau meant that he hadn't been starved as much as the other poor souls. Those people really suffered!

141

A few more miles along the road they came to another small house, where outside sitting at a little table were an elderly couple. In front of the table was a sign that read, 'Vegetables for Sale.' On the table were a few very old mangy looking carrots, a scrawny looking cabbage and one or two onions, which also looked well past their sell by date!

"Can we stop?" Peter questioned.

"Why not, of course," Rubin agreed.

As they left the car and approached the couple, Tom saw fear in their eyes. "Dad, they think we're the authorities. Maybe they think we are Germans."

"Please do not worry," Rubin announced to comfort the couple. "We saw the vegetables for sale and wondered if we might buy some."

As he said this, Peter looked confused. They had a whole basket of vegetables, bread and cheese in the car, all prepared that morning with love by Steph.

"How much for all of them," Rubin asked the woman.

"I can sell you the lot for twenty zlotys,'" the old woman replied.

"No," Rubin snapped. I cannot give you one zloty less than fifty."

"I accept your offer," said the old man, and he put the mainly rotten looking produce inside of a brown paper bag and presented it to the customer.

Now Peter understood what his friend was doing. He was helping these poor people by giving them money without them losing face by begging for it. He never thought it possible, but Rubin had gone up even higher in the youngster's estimation.

"Do you mind if we rest a while?" Rubin asked the couple.

The old man disappeared inside the house, returning seconds later with three stools. "Please," he said, gesturing for the three to sit.

They stayed chatting for almost an hour, during which time the couple told them about their war experiences, which thankfully hadn't been as bad as Rubin's, mainly for the reason that they had nothing for the enemy to steal from them.

"Have you ever heard about a camp named Auschwitz?" Peter questioned the couple. When they confirmed they had not, Peter showed them his tattoo – Two-Nine-Eight-Six-One.

The woman gasped as he told her about his war exploits during the sixteen months he'd spent incarcerated there.

"Good lord! How could these people do this to others?" asked the old woman, visibly moved by what she'd heard.

When Peter told her about his Margo and the reason they were heading to Krakow, she put her bony hand on his.

"I will pray for you, Son," she said. "I hope with all my heart that you find your Margo and have a wonderful life with her. After everything you've been through, the very least you deserve is to have a good life with the girl you love."

"Thank you," Peter said wistfully, "but I think she's dead."

"She is not dead, son," the woman smiled. "I know it. I can feel it in my old, creaky bones. Have faith. You will find her."

Ready to leave now, Rubin looked at the two boys. "Go and fetch the food basket from the car," he whispered to Tom, who duly obliged.

When he returned, Rubin took the basket from his son and put it on the table, also placing the brown paper bag full of the produce they'd purchased earlier by the side of the basket.

"This is for you," he announced to the old couple."

"What do you mean?" the woman asked, beginning to well up in her eyes. It had been a very long time since anyone had shown them any acts of kindness.

"Please accept this by way of a thank you for being so hospitable to us, and letting us rest a while in your charming

143

home," Rubin said to her. The elderly woman simply smiled at him in return.

Back in the car, Rubin asked the lads if they minded what he'd done. "I think we can go hungry for a day or two," he said to the two boys.

"Of course we can," Peter agreed. "But do you think Steph will be angry when she discovers that we have given all her food away?"

"Peter, Mum would be far angrier if she discovered that we hadn't given it to them," Tom laughed.

The other two quickly joined in with the laughter and soon all three were chuckling away together. They waved to the elderly couple and drove away.

Two hours later, as they entered Krakow they noticed many people aimlessly wandering around the city, or sitting in shop doorways looking lost and forlorn. These poor people, probably reasonably affluent at the outbreak of the war had had their homes confiscated by the Nazis for use by their own officers. They would not have been Jews, because as Tom pointed out; if they had been, they would not have survived but would have perished in one of the camps, probably Auschwitz.

"Have you been here before?" Rubin questioned Tom, fascinated by his son's knowledge of the history of Krakow.

"Yes," Tom admitted. "Actually this is where I came when I first left you and Mum on the farm. This is where I joined the resistance."

"So you know your way around the city?" Peter questioned.

"Not really, but it's coming back to me now I'm here," Tom revealed. "In fact, Dad, turn left at the end of this street and cross over the river. I want to show you something."

Rubin did as instructed, turning left at the next crossing. After a few hundred yards or so, they came to a long bridge crossing the river Vistula, which flowed through the middle of the city. They'd travelled a few hundred yards further when Tom made another suggestion.

"Stop the car, Dad, pull over just here." Again, Rubin did as he was told. "This is where they formed the Jewish Ghetto. They made thirty thousand Jews leave their homes and live here."

"Live where?" Peter asked in disbelief. "There's nothing here!"

Peter was correct in his assumption. All he and Rubin could see was a small square or courtyard, with one standing tap in the middle, and nothing else.

"That was their only water supply," Tom pointed out. "This was used for drinking and washing. Can you imagine?"

"How could thirty thousand people live here?" Peter gushed.

"Well not all at the same time. This was a stopping off place for the Jews about to be transported," Tom observed.

"Transported to Auschwitz?" Peter asked.

"Possibly," Tom returned, although more of a suggestion than a fact. "There are rail tracks not far from here, but I'm not sure where they head to."

"Poor bastards," Rubin offered. "Compared to these poor souls, my experience of war was a doddle!"

"We all suffered, Dad," Tom remarked in support of his father.

"So where do we need to go?" Rubin questioned his son.

"Turn the car around and head towards the old town," Tom instructed. "We need to go towards the 'Rynek Glowny,' the market square. I think we'll find the town hall somewhere close to this," Tom stated, and Rubin once again did as was instructed.

They soon reached the market square, where there was a beautiful old church as its focal point. All three revelled at its magnitude and were thankful it showed no signs of any damage. In fact, luckily there seemed to be no damage anywhere in the city. Sadly, the reason for this was that when the German troops entered Krakow in September 1939, the Poles surrendered to the enemy without any fight offered.

The good thing with this was that unlike other cities in the country, including Warsaw, the city retained all the beauty of the medieval place that it was, with its exquisite buildings and attractive open spaces.

However, the bad thing about the invasion was the fact that all these people now wandered the streets homeless, after suffering eviction from their homes without any chance of ever getting them back.

After parking the car, the three ventured into one of the numerous cafés dotted around the square. Once inside, Peter could imagine the place full of Nazi patrons demanding their coffee, beer or wine, or maybe a little 'quality' time with a pretty waitress or two! He imagined someone like Heinz Kappler barking out orders to the scared young women behind the serving counter.

Rubin ordered three strong black coffees whilst he asked the man behind the counter for information. "Are we anywhere near the town hall?"

"Yes you are," the barista replied. "In fact you are so close you should leave the car here and walk. It's only five minutes."

They drank the coffee, which they all agreed was disgusting, but then coffee beans were very scarce and Rubin thought these beans had probably been used before, after which they thanked the owner and walked in the direction they'd been instructed to take.

Soon they reached a building with a sign over the door reading, 'Ratusz.' Peter instantly began feeling nervous but excited at the same time as they walked toward the entrance.

They entered through a large, double oak door, which must have been ten feet high and eight feet wide. It was a grand entrance to an even grander building.

Inside, the floor was made of marble, with four marble columns stretching from floor to ceiling. The walls were adorned with magnificent artwork; paintings that Peter guessed had been saved from the Nazis by way of them commandeering the building to use as their own offices, until the surrender in May 1945.

This fact was later confirmed by Tom, who'had been active in this same area during his resistance days, although he did not elaborate on this any further, at least not in front of Rubin.

"Good morning gentlemen," they were greeted. "What can I do for you?"

The voice belonged to a well dressed man wearing black trousers and matching waistcoat, white shirt and black tie. Peter guessed that a black jacket would have completed the set, but at this time, the man was not wearing it.

"We need to talk with someone in the war records department," Rubin told the man.

"What do you need to talk about?" the man asked after removing his black rimmed spectacles and coming closer to speak more quietly.

"It's a very delicate matter," Rubin began. "This young man is Peter Florea, and he was in Auschwitz Birkenau for sixteen months."

"When did he come out?" the man asked.

147

"I left the camp on the twenty-fifth of January," Peter confirmed.

"Yes, but what year?"

"Nineteen forty-five."

"But that's impossible," the man said in disbelief. "Auschwitz Birkenau was not liberated until the twenty-seventh of January this year!"

"Yes I know that now. But I was taken out and put on a train two days before the liberation," Peter explained.

""Taken where?" the man questioned. "Where did they take you? Wait here," he said. "We need to go somewhere more private."

The man went off to find a spare interview room, leaving the three sitting there drinking in the opulence of their surroundings. He returned a few minutes later and asked Peter to follow him.

"Just Peter?" asked Rubin.

"Don't worry, I'll be okay," Peter reassured him. He stood up and joined the man, who now looked even more official as he was now wearing his jacket.

They walked along a corridor to the more private rooms of the building. As they did so, Peter thought about all the Polish residents of Krakow who may have been marched along these corridors scared witless, as they were about to face Gestapo interrogation!

They reached 'Interview Room 3' and the youngster followed the man inside. Waiting there was another official looking man with what looked like a book ledger on the desk in front of him.

"Good morning Mister Florea," the new man said. "Please may I call you Peter?"

"Of course," he confirmed.

"My name is Nowak and this is Mister Kowalewski," he informed Peter, whilst pointing at the other man in the room, the man who'd met them in reception. "Now I hear you have quite a story to tell?"

"Yes Sir," Peter replied.

"Before we begin, and I hate to have to ask this," Mr. Nowak said with honesty and sincerity in his softly spoken voice. "Do you have any proof of ever actually being in Auschwitz Birkenau?"

"Will this do?" the youngster said in reply. He then rolled up the sleeve on his left arm and revealed his camp tattoo, the tattoo that had scarred him for life. "This is my camp number – Two-Nine-Eight-Six-One - They did NOT use names in Auschwitz. We were no more than animals to those bastards!"

"That is barbaric!" Nowak said angrily.

Now he'd proved that he was indeed who he said he was, a surviving prisoner of Auschwitz, he had their complete attention. For the next hour or more, Nowak and Kowalewski listened in total reverence as Peter told his story.

They marvelled at his bravery, his courage and sheer will to survive, but above all this, the pair fell silent when he told them about his reason for being there today, the search for his Margo. They were both close to tears when he told them about the last time he'd seen her, that day when she'd left the camp at the mercy of Heinz Kappler.

"That is the reason I'm here," Peter divulged. "I need to look for her in case she is still alive. I will never give up until the day I know for sure if she is still with us or not."

"Do you have any details for her?" Nowak questioned.

"Her name is Margo Koval," Peter began. "The Nazis called her a Polish Jew, but she is, or was a Polish Citizen. Her camp number was Two-Three-Three-One-Two."

"Do you know where in Poland she was taken from?" Nowak questioned. "Do you know where she lived before the war?"

"Sadly not," Peter admitted. "We never spoke about our past lives, only our futures. We both thought that if we survived the camp, we would both walk out together. Well we did both leave on the same day, but not together," he said sadly.

"Two-Three-Three-One-Two you say," Nowak said. He opened the book and thumbed through a list of numbers. As Peter saw this, he became disheartened.

"How many numbers do you have?" he asked.

"There are about five hundred numbers here," Nowak replied. "These are all the Auschwitz survivors we know about."

"Five hundred," Peter shouted loudly in disbelief. "But there must have been three million people or more sent to the camp!"

"Sorry Peter, but these numbers belong to the people liberated by the Russians in January, and sadly many of these are dead now," Nowak admitted. "In fact you are the ONLY survivor I have ever met."

"So what can I do?" Peter asked sadly.

"Don't give up," Nowak replied. "You have come looking for Margo and if she's alive, hopefully she will do the same and look for you. I have added your name and number to the ledger, so if she comes here, I can pass on your information to her."

"Thank you," Peter said, obviously heartbroken.

"You are welcome to come here anytime," Nowak said, giving him a card with the address and phone number embossed upon it. "Now give me your details."

Peter, taken aback by this, told Nowak that he needed to ask Rubin for permission to give his address, and to use it as contact details.

"Of course you can use my details, Mister Nowak," Rubin replied when questioned. "Please do your best for this young man. He is one of the nicest young men you will ever meet, and he has been through hell. Please help him."

"We will do our best," the official replied.

Nowak and Kowalewski showed the three to the door and watched them leave. They both felt as though their lives had been enriched by meeting Peter.

Peter, Tom and Rubin left the 'Ratusz' and walked back to the car in silence. Then Rubin pointed out to the young man that it had not been a wasted journey. At least he now had the ball rolling, and if Margo were still alive, then she would find him.

"Come on. Let's get home," Rubin said, opening the door to the car.

"Yes," agreed Tom. "Let's go and have some of Mum's famous vegetable soup."

"With freshly baked bread," Peter laughed.

"With freshly baked bread," Rubin agreed.

They drove home mostly in silence, but as they drove past the house where they'd stopped that morning, Rubin began to laugh.

"Why are you laughing, Dad?" Tom asked his father.

"The lady is back sitting outside at the table," Rubin said smiling. "She has the sign there advertising that she has carrots for sale, and the mangy carrots she sold us this morning are back out on display again."

"I wonder how many times she's sold those carrots today," Peter laughed.

"Good for her, she's a business woman," Rubin smiled. "With cunning like that, it's no wonder she survived the war!"

# CHAPTER 18
# BUDAPEST

Over the coming months, Peter tried to visit Krakow at least once every few weeks. Luckily, Rubin was always happy to take him. However, the outcome was always the same, with no news of Margo.

"Sorry, Peter, but we have no news of her," was what he was constantly told by Mr. Nowak.

It was now Christmas 1945, but Peter did not feel like celebrating. In his imagination, he'd always presumed he would be celebrating this, his first Christmas in freedom with his beautiful Margo. As he sat waiting for the meeting with Nowak and Kowalewski, a thought entered his head.

"Mister Nowak, I have not been home to Budapest since 1943," Peter informed him. "Is there any way you could help me travel there?"

"I'll need to make a phone call," Nowak replied before leaving the room. He returned a few minutes later with good news. "Peter, we can organise the train journey for you. When do you wish to go?"

"I'm ready now."

"You want to go today?" Nowak questioned, slightly taken aback.

"Yes why not," Peter replied.

"I will see what I can do," Nowak informed the impatient youngster as he left the room again. He returned some thirty minutes later with papers for Peter. "You can use these anytime, but only once. One paper will take you to Budapest and the other will bring you back to Krakow. Do NOT lose them."

"Thank you," Peter smiled, but then he began to worry. What would the waiting Rubin think of his leaving. However, on that subject, he had no reason to worry.

"Of course you should go," Rubin reassured him. He then put his hand into his pocket and pulled out a fistful of money. "Here, take this," he insisted.

"I cannot take all your money," Peter said, almost apologetically.

"Peter, take the money and give me back what you do not use," Rubin ordered. "You cannot go all that way without cash in your pocket."

Rubin was correct of course, but it was still a marvellous and generous gesture, for which Peter thanked him.

"You must write to me and tell me when you are returning and I will come and pick you up from the station," Rubin stated.

"It's okay Sir," Nowak interrupted. "We will put Peter up in a guest house upon his return until you arrive. After what he's been through, it's the least we can do."

"Thank you," Rubin said to the very kind Mr. Nowak.

"Yes, thank you very much," Peter joined in. "And Rubin, please give Steph a big kiss from me and wish Tom a Merry Christmas."

The young man walked back to the car with Rubin, and then watched as he drove away.

He suddenly felt very alone. This was the first time he'd been without company since the day he escaped from the transportation train and crawled through the forest to reach the farm.

He waited until the car drove around the bend at the end of the road and was out of his sight, before making his way to the train station.

Peter was lucky because construction on the rail tracks between Budapest and Krakow had been completed in 1939, just before the outbreak of the war. Any damage to the line, if any, had long since been repaired.

Discovering the next train was to leave the station in three hours he decided to do what he always did every time he visited the city, which was to walk the streets for an hour or two and look for Margo.

He always thought that one day, whilst wandering the streets of Krakow he might see someone he recognised from the camp. Maybe he would meet another of the girls from the Kanada sorting room and they would tell him that Margo had survived. Maybe they even knew where she was living.

It was a good dream, but up until that day, it had never happened.


"All aboard," the railwayman shouted, as the train pulled to a stop on Platform 2 and after the passengers arriving, had vacated its carriages.

Peter stepped aboard and found a vacant carriage. However, he was soon joined in the carriage by a married couple. The woman looked at him and smiled, whilst her husband doffed his cap in his direction.

As Peter had been the first one inside, he was able to take a seat by the window and have a good look at the countryside as it passed by.

The distance from Krakow to Budapest was around two hundred and forty-five miles, so Peter estimated the trip would be about a twelve hour journey with all the stops the train would be making along the way, which didn't bother him at all.

Compared to the last time he'd taken a train out of Budapest, at least on this one he had the comfort of a seat and a window to look through. He was also sure the toilet facilities would be far superior to the two strategically placed buckets at either end of the carriage, as he'd experienced on the transportation to Auschwitz Birkenau.

As he looked out of the window at the beautiful countryside, Peter wondered if this was the same train line on which he'd made that journey during that fateful October afternoon, way back in 1943. Could this be the same view he could have enjoyed from the cattle truck had they had any windows to look through instead of the small crack in the wooden wall?

A man dressed in a well used, threadbare suit and peaked cap slid the door open and entered. "Tickets please," he requested.

The woman took two tickets from her handbag and passed them to the inspector, giving him the same smile she'd earlier afforded Peter. He clipped them, thanked her and handed them back.

As the official approached the young man in the window seat, Peter slid his hand inside the pocket of the overcoat donated by Tom and pulled out the official papers given to him by Mr. Nowak. He passed them to the railway worker, who looked very closely at the wording on the papers and then back at Peter.

"Thank you, Sir," he announced after a few seconds.

It had been a long time since anyone had called Peter, 'Sir,' in fact no one had ever called him 'Sir' before. It was obvious this ticket collector must have thought he was a very important person to have been presented with these official papers by the Krakow Ratusz.

He didn't know when it happened but at some time, he must have fallen asleep. When he woke a few hours later, the young couple had departed the carriage, to be replaced by a mother and two young children. He smiled at the little girl and she instantly shielded herself below her mother's dress. Peter laughed.

For some reason he reminisced about that day he'd been at the house of Heinz Kappler and thought about his children, Adolph and Eva. He wondered where they were now. Had they survived the liberation, and how had Kappler's lovely wife felt when she discovered she'd been married to a monster.

Although he worried about Frau Kappler and the children, he hoped that her husband, Heinz Kappler, was dead and rotting in Hell!

Stepping down from the train, a weird sensation came over him as his foot touched Hungarian soil for the first time in more than two years. Was that really all the time it had been, twenty-six months? In his mind, it seemed to have been a lot longer than that. To Peter, it seemed like a lifetime!

Compared to the last time he'd been here, the difference was huge. For one thing, he no longer had the big yellow 'Star of David' emblazoned on the lapel of his coat, advertising to all and sundry that he was a Jew. Today he felt anonymous, with no one jeering at him or giving him rude gestures, spitting at him, or even punching him as he walked along the road.

The city itself looked very different. He could see it had suffered much destruction whilst he'd been away. He hoped his family home had not suffered the same devastation.

Before the war, the young Peter enjoyed a very comfortable standard of living. The family lived in the Jewish quarter of the city in a large house close to the River Danube.

His father was a jeweller, making and selling jewellery in his own shop in the city. This shop was closed when German troops arrived to join the Hungarian army, immediately taking away the rights of all the Jews in Budapest.

Before this, although the Florea family would not have classified themselves as rich, compared to many others, they were comfortably well off. Peter had always intended in following his father into the business, hoping one day to run the shop himself.

Walking around the area where his family home stood, he noticed to his horror that the occupying enemy's dignitaries had now changed many street names. When he reached his old street, the name of it had been changed to 'Berlin Strasse.'

Peter instantly thought of Adolph Hitler and the Berlin bunker where he and his girlfriend, Eva, had 'supposedly' committed suicide.

How could they change the name of this beautiful street to one that just shouted cruelty, pain and genocide? He saw it as a personal insult to him and his family, as well as to all Jews, who before the war made up a quarter of the population of this once beautiful city.

Seeing his house for the first time in more than two years, he noticed it looked almost the same as when he'd left. He walked up the path and knocked on the door.

"Hello. Can I help you?" a strange man asked, whilst looking at him most studiously.

"I'm looking for my parents," Peter said confused. Who was this strange man?

"Well they're not here!" the man expressed indignantly.

"Well they should be," Peter expressed angrily. "This is their house!"

"I'm sorry son, but we bought this house in nineteen forty-three," the man said, a little calmer now.

"What month?" Peter questioned.

"It was October," the man confirmed.

"But who did you buy it from?" Peter asked, not wanting to give up in his quest for information.

"We bought it from the authorities," the man confessed. "They told us the people who owned it before couldn't keep up with the payments, so it was repossessed from them."

"That's a lie," Peter fumed. "My parents had long finished paying for this property. They owned this house and a shop in the city. They must both have been confiscated by the Nazis, and God only knows what happened to my Mother and Father." By now, Peter was incensed.

"What do you want here today?" the man questioned with obvious annoyance.

"What do I want? I want you to leave! This is still my family's house and I want it back!" Peter shouted.

Upon hearing this, the man refused to talk anymore and slammed the door in Peter's face.

The youngster turned and walked back down the path, a path he'd walked down thousands of times before, but this would be the last time. As he closed the gate behind him, he noticed a woman standing on the opposite side of the street. She was now staring at him intently.

"Peter Florea. As I live and breathe. Is that really you, child?" the woman asked with a puzzled expression.

Peter studied her. She looked familiar, but he was not too sure of her identity, but then recognition suddenly dawned on him.

"Misses Boszic, is that you?" he questioned the woman, not being sure.

"Yes, it's me," she revealed.

Peter took a good look at her. He observed that, sadly the war years had not been kind to her. Although only in her mid to late forties, she looked twenty years older. Her once beautifully managed black hair was now untidy, with lots of grey hairs bursting through. Her once perfectly manicured nails were now discoloured and chewed at the tips, and she was no longer dressed immaculately but now wore a dress that it must be said had seen far better days.

"How are you son?" she asked the boy.

"I'm okay," he replied. "But what happened to our house? There are strangers living there."

"Mister Hofstadter," the woman confirmed. "They are actually nice people, Peter. Don't be too hard on them. It's not their fault."

"But where are my parents?" Peter asked, desperate for information.

"Oh Peter, don't you know?" Mrs. Boszic said, but not really as a question. "The day after you left, the SS came along the street and did a sweep of all the homes belonging to Jews. They took them all away and we never saw any of them again."

"So I went through all that shit for nothing," he sighed. He knew that he would have been taken eventually, had he stayed, and possibly along with his parents.

"Your lovely mother and father were amongst those taken," Mrs. Boszic revealed. "I presumed they were taken to where you were being kept and they'd joined you."

"That might be truer than you think," Peter said sadly.

The realisation hit him that his parents could have been on the transport train a day or two after he had been. He imagined them in the cramped cattle truck and knew how difficult that would have been for them, especially his prim and proper mother.

They could have also been taken to Auschwitz Birkenau but taken immediately to the gas chamber and then executed upon arrival. He might have seen their ashes coming out of the crematorium chimneys, mixed up with others in that thick black odious smoke. He was heartbroken at the thought.

"Come in child," Mrs. Boszic offered, inviting him into her house.

160

"Thank you," Peter replied, appreciating the act of kindness.

Once inside, Mrs. Boszic asked him what had happened since the day she watched him walk down the road and hand himself to the mercy of the Nazis – 'voluntarily!'

She sat focused on his every word, as he told her his story of sixteen months in Auschwitz Birkenau! She hated, Heinz Kappler, and what he did to the lad, but she also fell in love with Margo.

"You have to find her, Peter," she offered, not really understanding the graveness of the situation.

The youngster told her about the help given to him by Mr. Nowak at the Ratusz in Krakow, Poland. Peter also told her that he believed that his beloved Margo had probably been murdered by the SS, and was now lying in a field somewhere close to Auschwitz. Mrs. Boszic was very sad at hearing this.

Peter continued with his story and when Mrs. Boszic heard about Paul Fuster and the way he'd spared the young man's life, she punched the air with excitement. She also fell in love with both Rubin and Steph.

"Oh Peter, you were so lucky to have found these people," she gushed.

"Yes I was, very lucky," he agreed. "They are now like a mother and father to me. I suppose even more so now," he sighed.

"I am so sorry for everything that has happened to you," she expressed, and he knew she was being very honest when she said. "We could do nothing to help your family that day when the SS came for them. If we'd offered any help, they would have shot us also, or taken us with them."

"I know that for certain," Peter reassured her.

"Now, do you have a place to stay?" she questioned.

"I was thinking to book into a guest house for a night or two," he replied.

"Nonsense," Mrs. Boszic cried. "You will stay here with me. It's the very least I can do."

"If you're sure," Peter queried.

"Peter, I insist on it," Mrs. Boszic replied, and then finished by saying. "And you are welcome to stay for just as long as you like."

That evening they chatted well into the night, not only about the war years, but also of happier times before the war. She reminded him of the happy times he'd spent with his family, also about what a loved and well respected family they'd been.

The one thing she did not mention was her husband. Where was he? What had happened to him? Peter didn't like to ask, thinking she would tell him if she wanted to.

"I expect you're hungry after your journey," Mrs. Boszic questioned. "I made this earlier and you are welcome to have some."

She presented Peter with a bowl of hot Goulash soup. As he tucked into the tasty bowlful of goodness, he thought of Steph and the vegetable soup she'd given him when he'd arrived that day. He actually felt guilty when he admitted to himself that Mrs. Boszic's Goulash was far better and much tastier that Steph's offerings.

After finishing supper, he was given directions to the spare bedroom, where he undressed, got into bed, and slept for the next ten hours! He must have been exhausted by the events of the day.

The next morning, after being gently woken by the sun streaming though the thin lace curtains, he dressed and made his way downstairs to be greeted by Mrs. Boszic holding a plate of cheese, salami sausage, ham and a big chunk of bread, all served along with a full pot of freshly brewed coffee.

"Breakfast Peter," she smiled.

After finishing his food and helping Mrs. Boszic clear away the breakfast things even though he'd been told to leave them, he made his way to the city centre. He wanted to see his father's old jewellery shop and see what had become of it, although in his heart he knew he'd be disappointed.

Again, when he reached the street, he could not believe the changes. All the shops in this area, before the war, had been owned by the Jewish community, but now, none of them were. His father's old jewellery shop was now a shoe shop, making, selling and repairing good quality footwear, with Mr. Salmat's grocery store next door now being a bakery.

Peter stayed rooted to the spot for a good few minutes, just looking at the frontage to the new business and remembering how it had been the last time he'd seen it. This time he decided not to go inside to confront the owner. He knew this would only end in another argument, and another argument he'd never be able to win.

Eventually he felt ready to leave and made his way to the banks of the River Danube, a place of solitude where he could sit for an hour or two and gather his thoughts. On the way to the river, as he strolled through the streets he studied the faces of every person he passed, but sadly he didn't recognise any of them.

Sitting there on the riverbank of the Danube, he watched the water as the sunshine sparkled and danced on its surface, putting him into a relaxed, almost hypnotic state.

Deep in thought, he realised he'd lost everything dear to him. He'd lost his parents, the family home, his father's shop and therefore his future employment. He'd had his freedom taken from him, with his youth stolen!

However, worst of all was the fact that he'd lost Margo, the most important thing of all.

Thinking now about the love of his life, he realised that had he not been imprisoned in the camp he would never have met her, so in a funny way, the sixteen months he'd been imprisoned in Auschwitz Birkenau were not only the worst months of his life, but also the best.

He decided that even if Margo was no longer alive, his life was still far better for having known her. He knew he would love her until the day he died, and no matter how long he lived, he would never find a woman he'd love more than Margo, the first love of his life. Sitting there on the riverbank, he felt very sad.

Suddenly he had an idea, a moment of clarity and a thought so clear in his head that he decided he must act upon it. He decided that he had to leave Hungary and Poland behind and begin a new life in a new country where nobody knew him. Before this however, he must retrieve his stash of jewels. He must return to Auschwitz.

He returned to the home of Mrs. Boszic and collected his belongings. After thanking and hugging her, he made his way to the railway station and waited for the next train to Krakow.

Two hours later, as he boarded the train, he consciously and deliberately left his foot on the platform a little longer than normal before lifting it onto the step and into the carriage.

He knew in his heart that this would be the very last time he would ever touch Hungarian soil again. His new life would begin – today.

# CHAPTER 19
# RETURN TO AUSCHWITZ

Arriving back at the train station in Krakow, Peter decided to head straight for the Ratusz, as he wanted to tell Mr. Nowak of his plans.

"But Peter, you cannot leave yet," the young man was informed. "We may need you to be a witness in the war crimes trials."

Nowak asked Peter if he'd heard about a man called Josef Kramer during his time at Auschwitz. He replied with the same answer that he'd previously given Rubin, stating that he didn't know of him personally but had heard stories of Kramer and another female SS officer, Irma Grese.

"Why do you ask?" Peer enquired.

"I can tell you that the two of them, along with forty-three other guards from Bergen Belsen have gone on trial in a place called Luneburg."

"Yes, I've heard about this," he told Nowak. "Rubin told me he'd heard it on the radio back in November. Apparently, as the camp was liberated by the British, they were tried under British law."

"That's correct, clever boy," Nowak stated, Peter thought a little patronisingly. "Well they found ten of them guilty of murder, including Kramer and Grese."

"Only ten," Peter queried. "What about the other thirty-five guards?"

"They all pleaded guilty to being there, but said they were only following orders."

"Yes, maybe they were, but they fucking enjoyed it!" Peter said with great emotion, but then apologized for this outburst. "Sorry for swearing," he said.

"No problem. It's understandable," Nowak replied. "Anyway, they haven't gotten away with it completely, as they were all given prison sentences ranging from four to ten years."

"That's all well and good, but they'll be in a prison cell far more comfortable than those which we were kept in. They will also not have the daily threat of death hanging over them constantly in their minds, for every waking moment of the day!" Peter was very angry now, which Nowak obviously recognised.

"Peter, I am happy that you're angry about this," Nowak claimed. "This is why we want you to stay here in Poland for a little longer. The Nazis and SS from Auschwitz One and Auschwitz Birkenau will be going on trial soon and as the only survivor I know, although there are more of you but not many, your evidence could be invaluable to the authorities. Would you stay for this reason?"

"But what would I do? I cannot stay on the farm with Rubin, Steph and Tom," Peter observed. "I would need to find work and a place to stay, and I will need money to stay."

"Leave that to me," Nowak told the lad. "We can find you something. It's the least we can do."

"But Mister Nowak, you have already done so many things for me, for which I am grateful," he replied. "Of course I'll stay if it helps."

"Good, One last thing," Nowak said grabbing the young man's attention. "Josef Kramer and Irma Grese are to be hanged in the town of Hamelin on Thursday the thirteenth of December. Do you wish to go? If you do, we will provide transport."

"Are you asking if I want to go and see them being hanged?" Peter queried.

"Yes," Nowak confirmed.

"No. I don't know them, nor have I ever seen them, so why would I wish to witness their execution?" was his answer.

"Okay," Nowak began, but was interrupted by the youngster.

"But if you ever find Heinz Kappler guilty of murder and have him hanged, please let me know," Peter pleaded. "I will put the noose around his neck myself and personally open the trapdoor! I would love to watch that bastard swing!"

Over the coming months, Mr. Nowak was true to his word. He kept his promise to the young man and found Peter work and accommodation so he could stay full time in Krakow.

The best thing was that the job he'd found for him was in the very café in the Old Town Square where Rubin had asked for directions that day, when they'd come to find the Town Hall and search for Margo.

The truly great thing about this employment was that because of the café's position, whenever he had time to spare, he could sit on the outside tables and watch all the people visiting the church or just relaxing in the square.

Peter concluded that if Margo was still alive, and it was a very small possibility, but if she was and she came looking for him, or simply came to visit Krakow as a tourist, the chances were that she would at least visit the square. She might even come into the café and ask him for a coffee, what a wonderful day that would be

Rubin and Tom took it in turns to visit once a month. By now, Rubin had taught Tom to drive so they could take it in turns to visit.

Sadly, Peter had not seen Steph for at least six months by now and he really missed her, especially her infectious laugh. She always sent him a kiss though, but this was not so desirable coming from Rubin or Tom! However, Steph promised she would visit him soon, and this always kept his spirits up.

He also looked forward very much to the cake she baked and sent to him every time Rubin or Tom visited, a lovely moist fruitcake. It tasted wonderful, but Peter decided it was definitely NOT for sharing!

Mr. Nowak came to the café every week to see Peter. He always brought the now expected news that not only was there no word on Margo, but also no visit from anyone else who may have survived the camp.

To be honest, Peter had given up any hope of ever finding her alive. He'd long gotten used to the idea that he was now all alone in the world. Although Steph, Rubin and Tom were like his family, they were not.

He was now simply waiting for Mr. Nowak to give his permission for him to leave Poland and begin a new life. However, one day he did receive some news.

"Peter, Rudolph Höss is about to go on trial at Warsaw," Nowak announced. "Would you like to go and give evidence against him?"

"I don't know," was Peter's honest reply. "What could I say?"

"The truth," Nowak replied. "Just tell the truth."

"But the truth is that I didn't see him do anything bad," Peter admitted. "I only saw him touch men on the shoulder at roll call, but why he did that, I honestly don't know. They were taken away, but I didn't see what happened to them."

"But you told me about the twelve Hungarian prisoners who were caught attempting to escape," Nowak reminded him.

"No," Peter said again. "I told you I'd been told about it by others who'd attended the roll call, but I wasn't actually there. Anyway, although he gave the order to Kappler, he didn't

168

shoot those poor men himself. Heinz Kappler did his dirty work!"

"But giving the order, that's as good as pulling the trigger," Nowak pointed out. "Anyway it doesn't matter. I'm sure there will be enough evidence to have that bastard hanged!"

"I'd like to see that," Peter said softly.

"That can be arranged," Mr. Nowak stated. "Don't worry about going to the trial, Peter. We can follow it on the radio."

"Thank you," the young man replied, thankful he did not have to face a roomful of his old tormentors. That would have been too much for him to bear.

The trial began in Warsaw on the 11th of March 1947. However, as most of the city was destroyed during the war and they were still in the process of rebuilding, the only place large enough to hold this trial was the auditorium of the Polish Teachers Union, situated in the Powiśle district of Warsaw. Even though it was the biggest building available at the time, it only had room to hold five hundred people, with many more wanting to attend.

Rudolph Höss was forced to stand and listen, as a lawyer read out the charges against him.

"You are accused of murdering three and a half million people. How do you plead?" the lawyer questioned Rudolph Höss

The defendant's reply repulsed everyone when he stated, "Not guilty. I only murdered two and a half million of the Jewish Pigs! The other million died of starvation and disease."

This statement brought gasps of horror from all around the auditorium, and probably also sealed the fate of the ex Auschwitz Birkenau Commandant.

Surprisingly, for a man as obviously guilty as charged, the trial went on for twenty-two days, however, the natural conclusion was finally reached on the 2nd April 1947, when Rudolph Höss was sentenced to death by hanging.

His date set for his execution was to be on Wednesday the 16th of April 1947 when he was to be hanged at Auschwitz Camp One.

When Nowak told him the details of the trial, when he mentioned the sentence and where it would be carried out, Peter's ears pricked up to attention.

"I have to go," he announced without hesitation. "I have to be there."

"Are you sure?" Nowak questioned. "I didn't think you'd want to watch him hang."

"It's not that so much," Peter admitted, "but the fact is that I might know some of the other ex-prison survivors who'll be there to witness the hanging. Maybe some of them might have news of Margo."

"Makes sense," Nowak agreed. "If you like, I can take you. Or would you prefer to go with Rubin, Tom, or both?"

Peter took a few seconds to think about how he should answer this question, but soon came to the conclusion that if he went with Mr. Nowak, it might be easier for him to be allowed into his old camp of Auschwitz Birkenau and therefore attempt to retrieve his stash of goodies.

"I would prefer it if you took me, Mister Nowak," he said, and then admitted the reason for the choice, that he needed his help to get into the old camp. He couldn't tell him the true reason why, but said that he wanted to go in there – alone – so he could remember and pay his respects to all the friends he'd had in the camp who hadn't made it, and had so cruelly lost their lives.

Nowak thought this was a perfectly normal thing to ask and told Peter he would not only take him, but he would also help him fulfil his request.

So on the morning of Wednesday the 16th of April 1947, Peter and Mr. Nowak set off in the dignitaries beautiful black Mercedes-Benz.

"The last time I was in one of these cars I was being taken to the house of Heinz Kappler," Peter observed.

"It may well have been this same car," Mr. Nowak replied, surprising the lad.

"What do you mean by that?" he questioned.

"What I mean is," Nowak began, "all the cars used by the Nazis were confiscated during the liberation of the camps and redistributed to us, the authorities in Poland. This could well have been Rudolph Höss's personal staff car," he laughed.

"Wouldn't that be ironic?" Peter said, also laughing at the prospect. "Imagine me travelling to Auschwitz to witness the execution of Rudolph Höss and travelling in his own car to see it."

They made great progress and one and a half hours later, the camp came into view. Peter was surprised at how close it had been to Krakow.

"I don't believe that in all the time I have worked at the café in the square, Auschwitz was only forty miles away," Peter claimed.

He also felt some strange feelings as he saw the camp looming close. However, this was only Auschwitz One, a camp he'd never been to or even seen before. He wondered what the sensations would be when he finally revisited and set eyes upon Auschwitz Birkenau for the first time since being marched out at gunpoint, two years and three months ago.

Nowak parked the car and he and Peter got out and walked the final two hundred yards or so to the camp. As they approached, for the first time ever he saw that sign above the entrance which read, "ARBEIT MACHT FREI," the sign which he'd read on the pamphlet in 1943, the same pamphlet which brought him here when he'd stupidly volunteered to come to the so called 'work camp.'

Nowak already knew the story of the youngster volunteering, so gave him a few moments to study the big metal sign before asking," Can you see the deliberate mistake, Peter?"

"Deliberate mistake? No," he replied, confused.

"Look," Nowak motioned, pointing to the sign. "When the Nazis ordered the Polish prisoners to make that sign, knowing it was a lie, they made it with an upside down letter 'B' in the word 'ARBEIT.' They knew that in this camp, work DOES NOT make you free! I wonder how many of the arrivals ever noticed this."

"Not many," Peter admitted. "They would all have had other things on their minds. Believe me, Mister Nowak, unless you experienced it, you would have no idea of what a terrifying place this was to arrive at, with guns pointing at you and dogs that wanted to tear you apart!"

"I can believe it," Nowak admitted. "Come on son. If you're ready, let's get in there."

There was a guard at the gate checking everyone had permission before allowing their entrance. Peter saw the funny side of this. The last time he was at Auschwitz Birkenau, there were guards on the gates to keep the prisoners inside the camp, yet now there was a guard checking to see if you were allowed to be let in or be kept out!

Approaching the guard, the youngster rolled up his left sleeve to reveal his credentials, his Two-Nine-Eight-Six-One tattoo.

"Thank you, Sir," the guard said. "Please come in."

"He actually called me Sir," he said to Nowak. "The last time I was in here they called me, Jew Dog, or Jewish Scum. Heinz Kappler always called me Jew Boy, but the man on the gate called me Sir." The youngster was ecstatic!

Inside the compound, Peter found he was one of around three hundred people here today, although they were completely unrecognisable from how they'd looked before as prisoners. These were the survivors of the Russian liberation, the prisoners left for dead by the retreating Nazis, who'd left the camp two days before the Russians had arrived.

On that day in January 1945, these people would have been skin and bone, just like walking skeletons. Now, after more than two years of medical supervision and literally being able to eat good food, they looked relatively normal again.

"Excuse me, do you, or did you know a girl called Margo Koval?" he persistently asked everyone he met, as he mingled amongst them. "Do you know if she's still alive?" he questioned. Sadly, his questioning was net repeatedly with silence and blank expressions.

"Never mind Peter, at least you know," Nowak said, trying to reassure him and offer a few crumbs of comfort.

"But I don't," Peter replied, angry at what his friend was insinuating. "I cannot believe my love is dead. I cannot give up on my search for her."

"But you have to give up and accept it if you want to begin a new life in a new country," the elder of the two insisted. As always, Mr. Nowak was the voice of reason.

"I suppose so," Peter conceded. "But I will never stop hoping. And I will never stop loving her."

As he walked around, Peter took a good look at this complex. The first thing he noticed was that, compared to Auschwitz Birkenau, this camp was constructed so much better and sturdier. Where Birkenau had been built of mainly wooden structures, the buildings in 'Camp One' were all constructed of brick, and therefore built to last.

The reason for this was that when the camp was originally built, it was erected for the sole purpose of housing detained Polish political prisoners and was a prison, not a death camp.

Auschwitz Birkenau was built later, when Auschwitz Camp One became too small to house all the Jews, gypsies and homosexuals who were being sent there.

Peter stopped outside Block 10, the place where Josef Mengele carried out his butchery. He felt a shiver run through him as he thought of all the children selected at arrival by the beast in the white coat for his experiments.

At the wall joining Block 10 and Block 11, he stood for a moment and prayed for all the people who'd lost their lives standing at this wall in front of a firing squad.

When he came to Block 24, the brothel, he thought of his beloved Margo, remembering the story she'd told him of when she'd waitressed at 'The Retreat.' He thought of her inside that block and enjoying the massive bath, where she and the other girls had enjoyed washing with soap and feeling clean for the first time in months.

He smiled as he touched the door and thought about Margo passing through it. He thought that touching something that she may also have touched made him feel very close to her.

Making his way to the place of execution, he looked up at the now empty watchtower and spotted the sign below it which read, 'Achtung Halt Juden,' standing in front of two electrified barbed wired fences, which were around ten feet between each other. In between these two fences was a stone gravel path, where the prisoners were forced to walk along on the way to their deaths!

Behind the second fence, Peter could see fields and could hear traffic as it passed by. He couldn't believe how close this camp was to civilization. Surely, the local people must have known the existence of this place and what was going on in here, but then he thought, maybe to admit to knowing would have been dangerous for them, so far safer to have turned a blind eye.

He finally reached the spot in front of a separate building that was once the Gestapo Headquarters, the offices where prisoners had been interrogated, with little or no chance of ever being seen again. In front of this building, a crude and temporary looking gallows had been erected specially for the execution of Camp Commandant Rudolph Höss.

The time finally came and a murmur was heard as the door opened and the diminutive figure of Rudolph Höss came shuffling out into the daylight. As a final insult to him, he was dressed in the prison uniform and not allowed to wear his SS officer's uniform.

Again, as he did at Kappler's home, Peter observed that out of that scary uniform, these men looked far less terrifying than they did when wearing that jacket with the swastika emblazoned on the arm. As he came closer, the soft murmurs turned into booing and hissing.

"Prepare to meet your maker," one man shouted.

"Say hello to the Devil, you evil bastard!" shouted another.

"Say hello to Hitler for me!" shouted a third.

One man simply shouted, "Why?" This was possibly the most poignant comment of them all.

Peter just stood there and watched. Although he hated this man almost as much as he hated Heinz Kappler, he had to admire his bravery. He was showing no sign of emotion or fear as he slowly walked towards the gallows.

Peter supposed this was possibly his last act of defiance, not to let the former prisoners see any weakness on his part. However, he later discovered that Höss had attempted to commit suicide in his cell, but was caught with a cyanide pill in his hand and stopped. So he wasn't that brave after all.

As he stepped up to the gallows, the hangman went to put a hood over his head.

"No, don't do that," a member of the crowd shouted. "Let us all see his face as he dies. We want to watch him suffer."

The hangman agreed to the demand and as requested, left Höss's face exposed for all to see. He took his last look around and then defiantly smiled at the waiting hoards.

"Any last words?" asked the hangman.

This was the final time that Höss could have redeemed himself and said 'sorry' to the people, but he did not.

"Sieg Heil," he shouted instead, and gave the Nazi salute.

The noose was placed around his neck, and after he stepped up onto a small three legged milking type stool, the rope was pulled tighter and the stool was then unceremoniously kicked from under him. He was then left dangling by his neck.

The crowd cheered as his body began to gyrate. This slowed down until only his feet were twitching. After jerking for a few more seconds, his feet twitched no more. A doctor was called for and he pronounced that Rudolph Höss was dead.

The crowd surrounding Peter instantly burst into ecstatic cheering and rapturous applause. However, Peter did not join in with these celebrations.

The day Rudolph Höss had been hanged at Auschwitz Camp One, he was only forty-six years of age, but was responsible for the deaths of three and a half million men, women and children. Not only this, but he was also responsible for unimaginable human suffering, the likes of which, Peter hoped would never be repeated in his, or anyone else's lifetime.

He stood for a few minutes quietly studying the lifeless figure dangling in front of him before Mr. Nowak broke the silence.

"How are you, Peter?" he gently questioned.

"I'm okay," Peter replied.

"Come on," Nowak said. "We have somewhere else to be."

The drive from Auschwitz to Auschwitz Birkenau only took a few minutes, but every second of the journey was painful for the boy. As they reached the gate, the youngster was visibly shaking.

"You don't have to do this, son," Nowak said, trying to reassure him.

"Yes I do," Peter replied.

Obviously, Mr. Nowak didn't know the real reason for Peter's visit and the youngster felt guilty for not telling him, but this was the one secret he had to keep, the one time when he trusted no one. Not even Rubin, Steph or Tom knew of his hidden stash, and he prayed it would still be there.

"Stay here," Nowak ordered. "I'll talk to the man on the gate."

There was a man sitting at a table at the entrance to Auschwitz Birkenau, again ironically there to keep unauthorised people out of the premises. Mr. Nowak approached the man and showed him his official identification papers. Peter then saw the two men deep in conversation.

"The young man sitting in my car is the only survivor of this camp I have ever met," Mr. Nowak began. "We have just witnessed the execution of Rudolph Höss and now he would like to come inside this camp to pay his respects to all his friends who died in here at the hands of the Nazis."

"But why would he want to revisit this place?" the man questioned.

"He has his reasons," Nowak confirmed. He then went on to tell the man all about Peter's life in the camp.

The man listened enthralled to the story of the lad's sixteen months inside this place, but when he heard about his love for his beautiful Margo, Nowak could see he was visibly moved.

"But there is no one in there. He will be totally alone," the gent advised.

"That's how he wants it. He just wants to walk around and remember his friends," Nowak repeated from the earlier conversation.

"Okay," the man agreed. "I can give him an hour."

Nowak thanked the man and returned to the car to give Peter the news.

The place had an eerie atmosphere, very creepy. Walking through the entrance, he couldn't stop himself from glancing up at the watchtower, half expecting to see a guard standing there with a gun pointing at him. Peter could not resist the temptation to take a closer look and climbed the ladder.

Inside the tower now, he was able to see the camp in its entirety and couldn't believe how massive it was, far bigger than he'd ever imagined.

He could also see the beautiful countryside surrounding the camp, making the whole existence of this place even more surreal.

Again, he thought there was no way in hell that local people didn't know about this place and the horrors going on inside. He observed that they must have seen the black acrid smoke belching from the total of five chimneys, including the one at Auschwitz Camp One, or smelled the putrid stench caused by it.

Peter also could not believe all the devastation to the buildings caused by the Russian liberators, many of the huts had been destroyed by these men setting fire to them. There was also lots of damage done to the Kanada building, but luckily, Peter could still make out the outlines of the foundations to where it stood. However, the gas chamber and crematorium five were no longer there as they'd been dynamited with the aim of removing all evidence of the killings. Peter imagined this must have been done on the day before the liberation, on the 26th of January 1945.

He climbed back down the ladder and made his way to his 'old home' and place of work – Kanada.

He traced his way around the foundations and eventually found what he thought was the alleyway between Kanada and the crematorium. He paced out the ten steps and then searched in hope for the little stone pebble. Suddenly there it was, he'd found it, the answer to all his prayers.

He fell to his knees and began frantically digging, as a dog would dig to search for a bone. Around six inches below the soil, he found the small canvas bag and began teasing it to the surface. Was it, or wasn't it? When he lifted the bag from the ground, he could feel by the weight that it contained something. Dare he look inside? His entire future depended upon the contents of this bag.

He waited for a few seconds and then plucked up the courage to look. The diamonds, gold necklaces and selection of gold and silver rings all sparkled back at him, as though they were saying, "Hello friend. Welcome back."

Peter was glad he was wearing his big coat. Although it was a reasonably warm day, this coat had deep pockets to hide the stash.

After doing this, he took a walk around the camp, stopping at Huts 27 and 44 to pay his respects to Franz, along with Oscar and the rest of the gypsies.

He went inside Hut 27 and it was like entering a time capsule. Nothing had changed. It was as though the inmates had just attended roll call and been marched off to the stone quarry to begin the day's work.

He made his way to the main square and imagined he was standing there with Margo, listening to the camp orchestra playing beautiful classical music. This made him smile. What did not make him smile, however, was the fact that the mobile gallows they used for the pubic hanging of prisoners had been left on full display.

Making his way back to the camp entrance, before leaving, he stood at the entrance to the Kanada complex and bowed his head in prayer.

"Dear Lord," he began. "If Margo is still alive, please keep her safe and bring her back to me, or at least help me find her – Thank you."

"All done," Mr. Nowak asked, smiling at Peter upon his return.

"All done," he confirmed.

"Where would you like to go now?" Nowak questioned.

"England," Peter replied. "I would like to go now to England."

# CHAPTER 20
## ONE CAMP TO ANOTHER

Arriving in the dead of night, Peter tried to look through the windscreen of the coach to catch a glimpse of where they'd stopped. All he could see was the pitch black darkness, broken up by the dim light of a small hut to the left.

He watched as a man came out of the hut to speak to the man behind the wheel. After looking at the driver's credentials, the man on the gate pushed down on the short end of the barrier, raising the long end high into the air for the coach to gain entrance and pass through.

As they drove past the hut, Peter could see the man more clearly. He was slightly concerned to see the man wearing a uniform, although this time it was a normal British soldier's uniform and not that of Hitler's Secret Service, better known as the 'SS.' But it was also comforting for the young man to later discover that this man's job was to provide security for those residents staying inside the camp.

They drove up a long drive until Peter began seeing huts on either side of the road, although these huts were like nothing he'd ever seen before. If you took a beer barrel and cut it in half from top to bottom then lay it down on the cut side, this is what these structures looked like.

He later discovered that these were formally air raid shelters now converted to house Polish refugees, along with one solitary Hungarian refugee, Peter, in a temporary makeshift camp.

After officially being invited to come into the camp, the thirty or more occupants of the coach were directed towards two huts. Once there they were told to find a bed for the duration of their stay.

Peter thought that the last time he'd had similar words to this spoken to him, they'd been spoken by the Sonderkommando on the night he arrived at Auschwitz Birkenau, but this was where the similarity ended. Here in this temporary shelter, they would be fed and watered, then given comfortable beds with mattresses. However, best of all was the fact that they had no fear of death hanging over them daily.

Peter looked around as he entered the designated hut. There were twenty beds per unit, ten on each side and facing each other. Between each bed, there stood a small chest of drawers to keep valuables. Peter was very happy to see that each arrival had their own key, so these drawers would be locked for safe keeping, so his jewellery stash would be stored reasonably safely.

He chose the bed at the far end of the long, narrow room, thinking that being the furthest away from the entrance there would be less chance of his being disturbed by the comings and goings of the other people in residency. He could also lie facing the wall, so giving himself a modicum of privacy.

After the long journey, sleep came easily for Peter, and he soon fell into a long and very deep sleep.

It had taken Mr. Nowak quite a few weeks to organise this new life for him, but because of all the troubles and heartaches Peter had been through, the authorities agreed to send the young man to England as part of the 'European Volunteer Workers,' via the UK Government Work and Settlement program. This was normally reserved for Polish nationals only, and eventually more than one hundred and fifty thousand Poles would come to live in various towns and cities across England, Scotland and Wales. However, there was a good chance that Peter was the only Hungarian to do so.

Waking the next morning and taking his first look around the camp, he felt blessed to be here, but also felt like he was back in Auschwitz Birkenau again. This was until he found his way to the food hall and had his first taste of English food.

After queuing in line, the very welcoming and happy looking women behind the counter took it in turns to put different items on his plate. When he went to sit at a table, he stared at the selection. There was a sausage; but it looked nothing like a Polish sausage, a rasher of bacon and slices of fried tomato. There was one very strange item placed on his plate, and something that he'd never seen before - baked beans! He looked at them with suspicion but gave them a go, finding that he liked them. Sadly, there was no egg on the plate, as apparently these were still scarce in England.

The lack of an egg instantly took him back to the farm, with Steph serving up her breakfast to him every morning. However, what he missed most about those days was the freshly baked bread she pulled out of the oven each morning. He deduced that the bread served in England was disgusting, pale white looking and tasteless!

Four weeks ago, Steph, along with Rubin and Tom came to Krakow to see Peter off and say their goodbyes. The farewell had been emotional, with Rubin, Tom and Peter trying to hold back the tears, but with Steph breaking down and sobbing uncontrollably.

"Promise you will come back and see us one day," she pleaded with the young man. Rubin and Tom also shared this request. Although he promised he would do so, in his heart of hearts, Peter was certain this would never happen and this would be their last ever meeting.

"If I am able to come back," Peter said bravely, "please don't attack me with that pitchfork again, Rubin." Hearing him saying this, brought a moment of humour to an otherwise tense and emotional situation.

"Look after yourself, Peter," Rubin said. "You know you are like a son to us."

"You ARE my brother," Tom added.

Steph summed it up in five words when she said, "We all love you, Peter." This was the sentiment that set them all off, and all four were now standing there blubbing together.

Again, Peter thought about that fateful day after he'd escaped from the transportation and woken the next morning with that pitchfork rammed into his leg. What a lucky boy he'd been that day. He would never forget their kindness for as long as he lived.

Peter was also very grateful to Mr. Nowak, who'd arranged this trip with the help and the organisation of the British Red Cross plus the British Army, who were providing the transport.

The arrivals at the camp were each given a few days to acclimatise to their new surroundings before being called in for an interview, not by the Gestapo this time, but an interview with a lovely person named Peggy.

"Hello Peter, my name is Misses Mountjoy, but please call me Peggy," she announced, with her wonderful smile putting the youngster at ease. "I'm here to help with your future life choices, where you'll be living and the type of work you'll be doing, etcetera. Tell me a little about yourself."

Well, for Peter there was no such thing as telling her a 'little' about himself, and Peggy sat engrossed to the lad as he told her everything. She couldn't believe the arrogance and cruelty of the Nazis, as he revealed his story about life in Auschwitz Birkenau.

"What happened to Heinz Kappler?" she questioned. He answered with a shrug of his shoulders. "I hope he was captured," she offered. "I hope they hanged the bastard!"

Peter was shocked at hearing her say this. She was such a lovely woman, middle aged and very prim and proper. In a way, she reminded him of Steph, because she had that same lovely motherly way about her, although she was not as overweight as his 'Polish Mother.'

"Peter, can you tell me of your plans for the future," Peggy asked. "Do you have any idea of the kind of work you would like to be involved in?"

"Before the war and before I went to the camp, it was always my intention to follow my father into the family jewellery business. However, when I went back to Budapest, I discovered the Nazis had confiscated his business premises, along with every Jewish business in the city."

"So you'd like to be a jeweller?" Peggy interrupted.

"Yes, very much so," Peter agreed, especially as he had a bag full of diamonds he wanted to cut!

"Leave it with me," Peggy announced. "I have a friend with his own jewellery business in the city of Bath. He might be able to take you on, but I can't promise."

"That would be great," Peter replied, really quite excited about the prospect, although he had no idea where the city of Bath was.

A few weeks later, Peggy called Peter to her office again. She had good news for him.

"I've been in touch with my friend. I have told him all about you and your story and he'd like to meet you for an interview. Would you be interested?" she asked.

"Yes, of course," Peter replied.

"Would you like to go and meet him next Wednesday?" Peggy questioned. "We can arrange transport for you." Peter agreed to all requests and thanked this lovely woman for her help.

The following Wednesday he caught the bus from outside the camp in Mangotsfield to travel the eight miles to Bristol Temple Meads, the train station situated in Bristol. He waited on Platform 9 until he heard the station announcer -

"The train arriving on Platform 9 is the eleven-twenty for London Paddington, stopping at Bath Spa, Chippenham, Swindon, Reading and London Paddington."

Before boarding the train, Peter asked a porter a question. "Excuse me, Sir, can you tell me how long the journey is to the city of Bath?"

"It's very short. Only twenty minutes or so," the uniformed man replied and Peter thanked him.

Boarding the train, Peter decided that as it was such a short journey he wouldn't bother to find a seat in a carriage, but would spend the journey standing by the door and looking out through the window.

He watched as the train sped past villages, countryside and farmland with cows and sheep munching on the grass, along with lambs frolicking in the fields. He thought it looked like a wonderful place to live.

However, if Peter was impressed by what he'd seen through the train window, it was nothing compared to the sights that greeted him upon his arrival in the city. The city of Bath was simply stunning!

Leaving the train and walking down the platform towards the steps to take him down to the ground floor exit, after stepping outside, he was happy to discover that unlike the station in Bristol, which was a little way from the city centre, this station, Bath Spa, was right smack in the middle of it.

Peggy had drawn a map for him to find 'Samuels High Class Jewellers,' the shop he needed to find for his interview.

He found the shop with plenty of time to spare, so thought he'd take a quick look around the area.

The shop itself was in an old street called, 'Abbey Green,' and situated three doors up from one of the oldest pubs in the city centre, a pub named, 'The Crystal Palace.'

In the middle of Abbey Green, surrounded by the cobbled stoned street was an island of grass with a huge oak tree in the middle. This tree was rumoured to be more than two hundred years old. This however, was not the oldest thing in the area, as just across the road from the shop was the Roman Baths, the place that actually gave the city of Bath its name.

There was a certain air about the place. Peter instantly felt at home here. He knew he could be happy living in this wonderful city. He made his way back to the shop and entered.

"Can I help you young man?" a very kindly looking man enquired.

"Hello Sir, I am Peter, Peter Florea," he announced, "and I have an interview with Mister Samuel."

"That's me," the gent replied with a smile. "It's very nice to meet you. I must say that Peggy speaks very highly about you."

"Thank you, Sir, she's a lovely lady," Peter smiled.

They say that first impressions are the most important thing about any meeting, and Mr. Samuel was already very impressed with the lad's politeness and good manners.

The interview seemed to be over in the blink of an eye, but the two were deep in conversation for more than an hour. Mr. Samuel was most impressed when told that as a boy, Peter worked in his father's jewellery business, and he showed genuine sympathy when hearing about the Nazis confiscating it.

He was also visibly upset when listening to the lad's story of his life in Auschwitz Birkenau. When shown the Two-Nine-

Eight-Six-One tattoo, Peter could see Mr. Samuel becoming angry, but his anger soon became subdued when hearing about Margo.

"I don't need to question you anymore, Peter," Mr. Samuel said to the young man. "I only have one more question for you."

"Yes Sir?" Peter queried.

"When can you start?" Mr. Samuel questioned

"Do you mean I have the job, Mister Samuel?" Peter asked excitedly.

"Yes you do," he answered, "I would be a fool to look for anyone else. I do have one more question to ask you though."

"Yes Sir?" the lad responded.

"Can you please stop calling me, Sir, or Mister Samuel and call me Harold?" the new boss requested.

"Certainly," Peter replied, now ecstatically happy. "And thank you...er...um...Harold," he said.

# CHAPTER 21
# FAIRGROUND ATTRACTIONS

It was now the summer of 1949. Peter had been living in Bath and working at 'Samuels High Class Jewellers" for more than one and a half years, with Harold Samuel being very pleased with his progress. He also personally liked Peter very much, as well as trusting him implicitly, so much so that Peter now lived in the upstairs accommodation above the shop.

The building itself was a three story Victorian property, a terraced house built in the mid 1800's. The ground floor had been converted into the shop at the turn of this century. Above the shop on the first floor, there was a living room, kitchen and bathroom, whilst the top floor housed two bedrooms and another separate toilet.

It was unusual at the time to have an indoor toilet, and indeed a bathroom, but as there was no garden at the property, this was essential. Peter loved it, as there was no need to brave the freezing cold winter temperatures if he needed a middle of the night pee. It was also far superior to the planks of wood he needed to squat over at Auschwitz Birkenau!

At first, Harold had given the young man a key to the side entrance at the shop frontage, but he now had access to the adjoining door directly from inside the shop. As well as being great for Peter, this arrangement was also good for Harold, as it meant that his insurance costs were greatly reduced. With Peter living on the premises, it was like having a full time live in security guard permanently on duty.

Peter had now reached the ripe old age of twenty-two, amazing when you think he should have died that night when he'd arrived in the camp at the age of sixteen, with only a lie about his age saving his life.

During the evening of his birthday, 23$^{rd}$ of May, by way of celebration, Harold took Peter for his first ever English beer in 'The Crystal Palace.' The young man enjoyed the ambience of the pub experience, but decided the bitterness of the ale was an acquired taste that he was not in any great rush to acquire!

One thing he really enjoyed about his birthday though was receiving a letter with a Polish stamp on the envelope. It was from Rubin, Tom and Steph. They'd written to wish him many happy returns of the day. Peter had read the letter every day for two weeks, and still looked at it from time to time, now three months later.

He was so happy to have kept in touch with his 'Polish family,' even though the frequency of the correspondence was not so frequent now. In the beginning, Peter wrote to them at least once a week, but the frequency of the correspondence had now reached once monthly.

He still loved receiving letters from them and learning about what was happening on the farm, likewise they very much enjoyed hearing about his life, where he was living and how the work was going.

In recent letters received, Steph kept asking when he was going to find himself a girlfriend, something that made him smile. However, even though it had been more than four years since that fateful day when he'd watched as Margo was marched out of the camp, he still felt that being with another girl would have meant he was being unfaithful to her. Stupid he knew, but it was how he felt.

During the third week of August, the funfair was in town. From Saturday the 20$^{th}$ until Thursday the 25$^{th}$ of the month, the fair was set up in Royal Victoria Park. Peter knew about this in advance, as Harold had been asked to put up a poster advertising it in the shop window. As he'd agreed to doing this,

Peter was given vouchers for some of the rides on the first night, so decided to go. They'd also given vouchers to Harold, but he thought at his age he was too old to use them, and so passed them on to his young compatriot so he could go on the rides twice, or perhaps he could share them with somebody else.

Closing the shop at six as usual, Peter busied himself to prepare for an evening of frivolity. After a good wash and brush up, he donned his favourite 'baggie' trousers and a crisp white shirt. At eight o'clock, he was ready, and left by the side entrance to walk to the park. He always left by the side entrance when going out, as he didn't want to carry the shop keys with him in public – just in case.

The first thing to hit him as he entered the fair was the smell of the onions frying at the hotdog stand. The intense aroma instantly made him feel hungry, but he thought about all that grease running down his freshly laundered shirt and decided that these hotdogs were something to eat on the way home, and not when first arriving.

Peter looked at the rides available and watched all the people, as they enjoyed themselves upon them. He found it fascinating to see people walking around with little bags of water containing goldfish. He wondered what these people would put them in when they arrived home, if they ever arrived home with the fish still alive!

He felt quite jealous as he saw girls walking around with their boyfriends holding them tightly. Many of these girls were carrying colourful stuffed animals or teddy bears, which the boys had spent a small fortune trying to win for them in a kind of darts game, where you had to place three darts into a playing card.

As it became darker, the fair came alive with its bright flashing lights and crescendo of noise, with distorted music played far too loudly blaring out through cheap speakers obviously not built for the job.

He watched the dodgems, laughing as he noticed the young male attendants jumping from car to car and hanging on to the poles that connected them to the electric. He noticed how they only jumped onto the cars occupied by the pretty girls, flirting with them mercilessly. He deduced that it must be a great life for these lads, travelling around the country and being in a different place every week with different girls to flirt with, although he also wondered what kind of success rate they had.

For some reason he was attracted to the carousel. He couldn't take his eyes off the roundabout with the colourful horses bobbing up and down, seemingly in time with the music. Of all the rides this was probably the most gentle, so why did he find it so hypnotic?

He noticed two pretty girls enjoying the ride. They were laughing together as they were sent into the air and then down again on the wooden horse, their long hair flowing in the breeze as they leaned back on the upstroke. Peter loved to see these two young girls having fun.

He watched as the ride began to slow, eventually coming to a full stop. The people removed themselves from the wooden horses and stepped down the three steps taking them back to terra firma. Then it was the girls turn.

As he stood there, one of the girls tried to negotiate the steps but lost her balance and started to fall. Peter sprang into action and ran to her aid. Reaching the second step, she lost her balance completely and began stumbling uncontrollably, but he was there by now and he caught her, just in the nick of time.

"Thank you kind Sir." she smiled. He looked at her. She had beautiful eyes. "What's your name?" the girl asked.

"I am Peter," he replied, with her noticing his foreign accent.

192

"Where are you from, Peter?" she questioned.

"I'm from Hungary," he revealed.

"Oh! I've never had a Hungarian boyfriend," she laughed. "My name is Jayne and this is my friend Rose."

"Nice to meet you girls," Peter said addressing the pair.

The three spent the rest of the evening together. Peter gave his 'double' vouchers to the girls and he enjoyed watching them having fun together on the various rides.

"I'll be going now," Peter said later as he was about to leave. "Thank for a lovely evening you two. I have really enjoyed your company."

"So what time are you going to meet me tomorrow?" Jayne asked brazenly, shocking Peter with her frankness. He also noticed that Rose was not a part of the equation.

"You want to see me again tomorrow?" the young man queried.

"Yes of course, you're nice. I like you," Jayne admitted.

They arranged to meet the next afternoon, when Peter took Jayne to see a movie at the Odeon Cinema in Southgate Street.

This was the beginning of a twenty-one year romance. Even though he thought he could never love her as much as he loved Margo, he gave her as much love as his heart possibly could. Anyway, Jayne was here and Margo was a ghost, although he still felt guilty for loving Jayne, as if he was being unfaithful to his beautiful Margo, but whatever happened, he would NEVER forget her, or her memory.

One year after their first meeting and almost to the day, on Saturday the 19th of August 1950, twenty year old Jayne and twenty-three year old Peter were married. After a short honeymoon staying in a guest house at Weston-Super-Mare, with Harold's permission, Jayne moved into the accommodation above the shop with Peter. In the previous year, Harold had gotten to know Jayne very well and very much approved of Peter's choice of bride.

"She is a lovely girl, Peter," Harold had said. "She will make a good wife for you, I'm sure."

Eighteen months later, the family expanded when Jayne gave birth to a baby girl in February 1952. When Peter first met his daughter, he thought he was going to explode with joy.

"Can we call her Margo?" he asked his wife. Jayne agreed without asking any questions.

Peter had told her about being sent to the camp and also shown her his tattoo, but he'd never spoken with her about Margo. He thought it would be unfair for her to have to compete with a ghost. He was still relieved when she agreed to his request and the girl was given the name, Margo Florea.

Florea – This was something else that he'd considered changing. When he arrived at the Polish camp in Mangotsfield, Peggy had asked him if he would like to 'anglicise' his name, changing it from Florea to Flowers. Although he thought about it, he decided that if his love had survived the march that day and was looking for him, the change of name could confuse any search, so he kept his original name. Anyway, Jayne always said she liked it.

"Jayne Florea," she'd laughed when the Marriage Certificate was signed by the couple. "I like it. It sounds kind of regal."

They had a good life together, a life full of love. Little Margo had grown into such a happy child and was a joy to her parents.

Harold also loved her very much and Margo called him, Grampy. This was wonderful for Harold, as he'd never married so had no children, or grandchildren of his own. He had for a long time considered Jayne, Peter and now little Margo to be his family, and he loved them all.

One day during the summer of 1957, the shop was open as usual but Harold seemed different for some reason. Peter asked if there was any problem, and was intrigued when the elder man replied, "Peter, can we have a talk when the shop closes?" Peter agreed, but worried for the rest of the day.

"Peter, I'm getting old," Harold began a little later. "I am too old to be doing all this work for too much longer."

Peter was very worried now. Was he about to close the shop and put Peter out of work? He would also have nowhere to live. The answer to this question could not have been more opposite to his thoughts.

"I want you to run the business as though it's your own," Harold revealed.

"What do you mean?" questioned a confused Peter.

"You are like a son to me," Harold replied. "I have no real family, no wife or children, but I have always considered you as my family and I want you to have the shop. My home at Lansdown has been long since paid for, and this building is also owned outright. I have a good amount in the bank, at least enough to support me in a happy retirement."

"But...." Peter tried to say, but Harold ignored him and continued.

"Peter, I want you to take over the business and run it as your own. You employ the staff, pay the wages and buy the stock. You already make the jewellery, so buying what you need will be no problem for you. All I ask is for you not to change the shop name, and maybe give me a little pocket money each week."

"Can I employ Jayne?" Peter asked Harold.

"Of course," the elder man replied. "You can employ anyone you wish. It's your business."

"Deal," Peter smiled. They shook hands and Peter, at the ripe old age of thirty years was suddenly a business owner in the city of Bath.

Life could not have been better for the Florea family. Jayne had given up her part time job at 'Marks & Spencer' and now helped Peter in the shop full time.

Little Margo was about to begin school, so Jayne was able to take her and collect her each day, which would have been far more difficult, if not impossible, if she was still at her previous employment.

Peter had taken on a girl to work part-time on a Saturday, helping to serve customers at the shop. Her name was Wendy. She was a very nice girl and a pretty young thing. She was at the age when about to leave school and go to college.

Whenever he looked at Wendy, Peter marvelled to think that this really young looking girl would be about the same age as he and Margo had been when in Auschwitz Birkenau! He wondered how he'd ever survived.

He was also now about the same age as Heinz Kappler would have been then, and he wondered how Kappler could have treated them so badly at that time. There was no way in the world that Peter could be so cruel to Wendy. Kappler must truly have really been a monster!

Business continued to flourish, giving Peter, Jayne and little Margo a good standard of living. Harold still popped in from time to time to talk about the business and offer any advice needed. Just recently, however, Peter noticed that his old mentor was not looking too well.

The Florea family had reached the 'swinging sixties,' but Peter received the bad news in the autumn of 1962. A police officer entered the shop and looked at Peter.

"Excuse me Sir. Are you Peter Florea?" he questioned.

"Yes," he answered, wondering why there was a police officer in uniform standing in his shop.

"Do you know a man named Harold Samuel?" the man in the uniform asked.

"Yes – Yes I do," Peter confirmed. "Please tell me what this is all about."

"I am very sorry to tell you, Sir, but Mister Samuel has been found dead in his home."

"What? – How? – Why? - When?" Peter had all sorts of thoughts spinning around in his brain.

"He was found today sitting in his armchair, having suffered a massive heart attack," the officer revealed. "His neighbour became concerned when she noticed the bottles of milk had been on his doorstep for two days and she phoned us."

Upon hearing this, Peter felt lost. The officer could see in his face what he was thinking. "Don't blame yourself, Mister Florea; there is nothing you could have done,"

"Yes there is," Peter demanded. "I knew he wasn't in the best of health, so I could have checked on him more often."

Over the next few days, Peter could not shake off the feelings of sadness. Death was nothing new to him. He'd witnessed literally hundreds of thousands of deaths in the camp, some of them good friends to him, but this was the first ever death by natural causes he'd ever experienced.

Harold was actually older than Peter had thought. He was shocked to discover the old man was in his late seventies – ten years older than Peter thought he was.

The funeral took place two weeks later at Haycombe Cemetery, with the church being standing room only.

Although ten years old now, Jayne and Peter decided that little Margo was still too young to be subjected to death and a funeral, so Jayne stayed at home to take care of her. They closed the shop for a few days as a mark of respect.

As they lowered the coffin into the freshly dug grave, Peter thought of his lovely Margo, was his beautiful girl buried in a shallow grave somewhere in Poland, maybe in a forest close to Auschwitz?

"Excuse me Sir, are you Mister Florea?" Peter looked at the man asking the question, a tall thin man wearing a 'Crombie' overcoat.

"Yes," he confirmed.

"My name is Mister King and I am, sorry, I was Mister Samuel's solicitor for many years. Could you please come to my office tomorrow morning at ten?"

"I'll be there," a confused Peter agreed.

The next day, Peter dressed in a smart suit and took the seven minute walk to Mr. King's office in Chapel Row, situated just off Queen Square. He was surprised to find himself alone, with no one else in attendance.

Mr. King was dressed slightly less formally today, but was still wearing the regulation solicitor's pinstriped suit they all seemed to wear. Peter didn't have to wait long before discovering the reason for his summons.

"This is Harold Samuel's last will and testament," he announced. "He has left everything to you. His shop premises, his house in Lansdown and all his money."

"Are you joking?" Peter suggested, as his legs began to give way below him.

"No Sir," Mr. King replied. "You, Mister Florea, are a very wealthy man."

The inheritance made no difference to the Florea family's lifestyle, with Peter remaining to be the same hardworking man he'd always been. He did consider selling the house in

Lansdown, but could not bring himself to do so. He thought about how hard Harold had worked to buy it, and so to sell it for profit, he thought would have been an insult to his memory. Instead, he decided that as Harold considered young Margo to be like his granddaughter, he would give the house to her when she was old enough to move in.

Talking about young Margo, well, she was not so young anymore. It was now 1968 and she was just about to take her 'O' level exams as a beautiful sixteen year old. Jayne was very proud of her daughter, and Margo was the apple of Peter's eye. She passed her exams with flying colours and her parents persuaded her to remain at school to take her 'A' levels.

Again, Peter looked at her and couldn't imagine that she was now the same age he'd been when he was sent to the camp! He was so young at that time and was sure that he was not as mature then as his daughter was now.

The swinging sixties finally came to an end, with 1970 arriving. This would be a significant decade for the family, and not all for the good.

Peter noticed that Jayne was not her usual bubbly self. She lacked energy and seemed lethargic. When she kept falling asleep in the daytime, he suggested she make an appointment to see their doctor. They went together a few evenings later, after first closing the shop.

Doctor Colemain at the St. Marks Road Surgery was not happy with Jayne. He made an appointment for her to go for a more detailed examination at the Royal United Hospital in Weston, an area of Bath where the hospital was.

Two weeks later, Peter took his wife to see the consultant for a quite invasive examination, which although unpleasant for Jayne, it had to be done. They received an appointment to return two weeks later to receive the results.

"Mister and Misses Florea, please come in," Doctor Bliss greeted, gesturing for them to come inside a room with comfortable furniture and pale pastel coloured walls.

When he'd examined her two weeks earlier, the doctor had worn his green surgical uniform, but today he was dressed in the normal doctors long white coat.

For some reason this sent a shiver down Peter's spine, as it reminded him of Josef Mengele. Why he'd thought about him, he did not know. He'd not thought about the 'Angel of Death' at Auschwitz for at least twenty-six years. However, for what Doctor Bliss was about to say, it may as well have been Josef Mengele sitting there and giving the prognosis!

"There is no easy way of saying this," the doctor began, "but you, Jayne, have a very rare and progressive form of cancer, for which, at this moment in time there is no cure." He waited a few seconds to let them digest the news before continuing. "But with all the medical advances, who's to say we won't find a cure very soon."

"Maybe, but it will be too late for my wife," Peter said angrily.

"Please don't lose hope, Mister Florea. It goes without saying that we will do everything in our power to keep your wife comfortable and as pain free as possible," Doctor Bliss instructed. "May I suggest that you enjoy whatever time you still have together?"

"And how long do you think that will be?" Peter questioned.

"I don't know," Doctor Bliss answered honestly. "It could be weeks, months or maybe a year, but I don't think it will be more than a year."

"This is ridiculous," Peter raged, slamming his fist down on the arm of the chair. "They can put a man on the moon but they cannot find a cure for cancer! What kind of a world do we live in?"

Jayne Florea died on the 16<sup>th</sup> of May 1971. She died in the Forbes Fraser private hospital in Combe Park, in the Newbridge area of Bath. She had Peter and daughter Margo sitting either side of the bed, with each holding a hand. Sadly, Jayne was so pumped full of morphine that she didn't know they were there, but at least she died pain free.

For the first time since that first day on the farm when he'd met Rubin and Steph, Peter cried like a baby. He didn't cry for too long, as he had to stay strong to take care of Margo. The child was devastated at losing her mother, who was also her best friend.

It was a beautifuly sunny day when Jayne was laid to rest at Haycombe Cemetery. She was buried not far from Harold's resting place. The funeral took place on the 27<sup>th</sup> of May, four days after Peter's forty-fourth birthday. She was only forty-one years of age.

That night when Peter arrived home, the loss really hit him. The place seemed empty and he felt very alone. Even though he had Margo there to comfort him, she was no substitute for the loss of Jayne.

What would he do without her? If he'd been a drinking man, he would have drunk himself paralytic, but since that time when Harold had taken him to the pub on his birthday and he'd not liked the taste of the beer he'd left it alone, preferring the taste of an ice cold soft drink.

All of a sudden, through his mixture of anger and sorrow, he knew what he must do. He went to the shop safe and took out a canvas bag full of gold and silver rings, necklaces, bracelets, diamonds – and THAT diamond – the first he'd ever stolen in Kanada.

On many occasions, he'd taken the bag from the safe to look at the booty inside but had never had the heart to sell them. Although he was really stealing them from the Nazis as they'd already stolen them from the victims, he still felt as though to sell them would be all kinds of wrong.

Those people had believed when they'd carried them into the camp that night that their jewellery would be used to barter for food, NOT for Peter to make a profit. However, he made the decision that the time had now come.

The next day he set about cleaning them, highly polishing them as only a jeweller can. The rings, necklaces and bracelets sparkled like new and were all put on display in the most prominent part of the shop. The complete selection were sold in no time.

The diamonds, with which he'd intended to use to make rings or necklaces, he also polished, but not to sell in the shop.

The following Monday he took all the diamonds, except the big one, the first he'd stolen and the biggest diamond he'd ever seen, to London. He went to the diamond center in Hatton Garden, where a very good offer was made, an offer that he accepted.

The next day, he took all the money he'd made from the sale of the diamonds and the stolen jewellery to the hospital where Jayne had passed away and gave it to them, donating thousands of pounds to Cancer Research. In return, the hospital changed the name of a section of the hospital to, 'The Jayne Florea Memorial Wing.' At least something good had come from his time at Auschwitz Birkenau.

Over the next few months, Peter could not face life. He realised that now he'd lost Jayne and Harold, although he had

202

lived in England now for many years, he did not consider himself to have have any real friends in this country. He had many, many people who admired him, but he'd never let any of them become close, and didn't understand why.

He spent each evening sitting alone upstairs in the shop, sometimes he had the television on but was not watching it, sometimes he just sat in silence in his armchair holding THAT diamond in the palm of his hand. When he did this, he squeezed it hard until it hurt. Feeling the pain made him think about his time at Auschwitz Birkenau and remember his beautiful, Margo Koval, the girl he admitted to still loving.

Should he be having these thoughts about his lovely friend from the camp? He had not long buried his wife, Jayne, so why was he constantly thinking about Margo? Was he being unfaithful to the memory of his deceased wife by thinking about his beautiful friend from the camp, or was it the case that during his twenty-one years married to Jayne, all that time he was being unfaithful to Margo?

One thing he did know though, was that the diamond he held within the palm of his hand was worth more money than most people would ever see in a lifetime. With his home, business and all his money, he was a very wealthy man, but sadly no longer a happy one. He decided that if he had the chance he would give it all away in a heartbeat, if he could have one more day with Jayne, or Margo, or both.

Gradually he pulled himself together and got his life back on track. His daughter had decided to leave school and go to college in Bristol.

Peter thought about travelling on the train to see his daughter for a day and visiting Peggy, the woman who'd really helped him when he first arrived in the country. He thought about how nice it would be to introduce his daughter, Margo to her, as well as thanking her for giving him the life she had done for him. However, he discovered that the Polish Refugee Camp at Mangotsfield had only been a temporary structure and had long since had a housing estate built upon it. Because of this, sadly there was no way of finding out how to contact Peggy.

At the beginning of 1972, the business was again doing very well. After the slump he'd let it get into after Jayne's death, Peter had pulled it around, so much so that with Margo away studying, he could no longer manage the place alone and needed to take on staff.

He held quite a few interviews but when Andrew walked into the shop, instantly the position was no longer vacant. This young man reminded Peter so much of himself when he was at that age. He liked the young man immensely and was sure he could trust him, which of course was extremely important in the jewellery business.

Margo also agreed with her father and thought that Andrew was a lovely young man, so much so that within two years, at the age of twenty-two, she married him. Two years later, their family was complete when she gave birth to a baby daughter who they named, Grace.

It was now 1976 and at the age of forty-nine, Peter was now a grandfather. This was amazing when he considered that he should never have reached his seventeenth birthday, let alone his forty-ninth!

A few months before his fiftieth, Margo came to see him. She'd been thinking about what she could do to make his big milestone birthday special, and she had a suggestion she hoped he would like.

"Dad, for quite some time now, Andrew and I have wanted to visit Paris for a few days," she began. "We thought we could go on the weekend of your fiftieth birthday and that you'd like to come with us?"

"Why, do you need a baby sitter?" Peter said, but he was only joking. "Of course, sweetheart, I would love to come."

"It means we'll have to close the shop," Margo stated.

"That doesn't matter," Peter observed. "It doesn't mean we'll lose money, it just means we will be delayed in getting it."

And so on Sunday the 22$^{nd}$ of May 1977, the day before Peter's fiftieth birthday, the family, Andrew, Margo, Peter and little Grace, all made their way to Bristol Airport to catch the flight to the Paris Charles de Gaulle Airport for their five day break to the French capital.

Unknowingly to them, especially to Peter, this trip was going to be both eventful and unforgettable!

# CHAPTER 22
# THE BEAST OF PARIS

"Good morning Ladies and Gentlemen. Welcome to the ten-fifteen flight to the Paris Charles de Gaulle Airport" the soothing and reassuring voice of the pilot announced.

Forty-seven minutes later, the family touched down in France and made their way to the arrivals lounge to meet their arranged transport, which had been sent by the hotel they'd booked.

They were staying at the 'Hotel de Paris' in Montmartre, the artist quarter of the city, aptly named because of the extreme beauty of the area, which drew artists from all over the country, if not the world, to paint the picturesque scenes.

After checking in, they went to their separate rooms, but not before arranging to meet one hour later in the same spot of the hotel reception.

"We're only here for five days, so plenty of time to rest when we get back home," Andrew joked.

An hour later, they assembled and left the hotel to explore the city. They thought it would be a good idea to take a river cruise on the Seine, as this would take them past all the famous sights of the city and they could make a mental note of where to visit the next day.

They sailed past the Notre Dame Cathedral and could see the Eiffel Tower in the distance. However, little Grace was more interested in the fish swimming in the clear water. At this moment, she was trying her best to get to them.

Peter had to cling on to her for dear life to stop her wriggling free and falling in. For the first time in a long time, he was having fun. He only wished Jayne could have been here to enjoy it with him.

They returned to the hotel some five hours later. Margo, Andrew and Grace went to their room for some rest and relaxation, whilst Peter announced he wanted to take a slow stroll around Montmartre.

On his walkabout, he stopped to look at the artists with their fancy easels and highly coloured oil paints, marvelling at some of their work. Peter always carried a photo of Jayne with him, a picture of her in her younger days and thought about asking one of these men to paint a portrait of her for him. Sadly they all told him the same, it would take longer than the five days to complete, and so Peter made a mental note to return here again in the future and get the job done.

He went off the beaten track, avoiding the tourist path and wandered down the side streets, alleyways and walkways to find the real Paris, where the real Parisians lived. He entered a little Parisian café and was soon in conversation with the owner.

"How was it here in Paris during the war, when the Germans occupied France?" he questioned with great interest.

"After the initial few weeks when they wanted to establish their superiority and bossed us around, it settled down to be not too bad," the café owner and head barista informed him.

He went on to say the troops and officers alike were all told from way on high that whenever they frequented any businesses, whatever they consumed they had to pay for.

"If they came into this café," Michelle told Peter, "if they had a Café au Lait, it was paid for. If they drank a beer then they paid for it. They were always polite and never any trouble for us, as I say, after the first few weeks."

"So very different from my war experiences," Peter told the Frenchman. He then told Michelle about his time in the camp. The man listened to Peter's war stories in horror.

"I am so sorry for you," Michelle said upon hearing the end of the story, or as much as Peter wanted to reveal. "It sounds like we were very lucky here in Paris. As long as we caused no threat or trouble for them, they treated us well and integrated with us, even becoming part of the community, so much so that at the end of the war, many of the occupying officers returned to Paris and have lived here with us for many years."

Hearing this put Peter in a rage, the very thought that he could be walking down a Parisian walkway and sharing the pavement with a man who had once been his enemy, he found repulsive.

After thanking Michelle and leaving his café, Peter found himself studying the face of every man he saw as they passed him, wondering if they had once been wearing the uniform with the swastika on the arm.

He couldn't believe that even after thirty-two years had passed since leaving Auschwitz Birkenau, he still had an unforgivable hatred for those people. There was one man, however, that he had nothing but respect for, an SS officer named Paul Fuster, the man whom Peter owed his life.

A year or so after Auschwitz Birkenau had been liberated, and at about the same time as Rudolph Höss had been put on trial, when Peter told Mr. Nowak about his great escape, also about Paul Fuster's major part in it, he'd asked Peter if he would like to write a letter of support for the young man.

"It could be used by the defence team at Fuster's trial," Nowak had told Peter.

Peter had written this letter for Paul without a second thought, and often wondered what had happened to him. He hoped it had saved his life, as Paul Fuster had saved his. Maybe he would meet up with him in the next Parisian café he visited. That would be nice.

Before leaving the family, Peter had agreed to babysit little Grace this evening so that Andrew and Margo could go out for a romantic evening. Romance was of course, what Paris had been built for.

Before returning to the hotel, he popped into what looked like a nice Parisian eatery and ordered an entrecote steak and fries, with a side order of salad, accompanied with a boat of 'Sauce Chasseur.' It was wonderfully tasty, prepared as only a French chef could produce. It set him up nicely for his evening of reading stories and playing games with granddaughter, Grace.

The next day they visited La Louvre Museum, where art lover, Peter was excited to see the 'Mona Lisa.' However, expectation was better than reality. Although he thought it a beautiful work of art, he couldn't believe how tiny it was when compared to many other works in the museum. It was only around eighteen inches in height and encased in a highly alarmed, protective glass case, which meant that visitors could not get anywhere close to it – very disappointing.

From La Louvre they walked to the Eiffel Tower. This was a two mile walk, too far for little Grace's legs so Andrew and Peter took it in turns to carry her on their shoulders. Even though Margo still had her pushchair to push everywhere they went, Grace screamed the place down when her mother tried to sit her in it. No, she wanted to stay on Granddad's shoulders!

Late afternoon they walked up the Champs Élysées to see the famous 'Arc de Triomphe.' Peter had seen photos of this taken at the beginning of the invasion, depicting the German army goose-stepping into the city to begin its occupation in June 1940.

The sight of the structure sent shivers down his spine as he thought about how terrified the Parisian residents must have been at seeing this war machine invading their territory and their lives. It was very sad that this magnificent, historical building was now in the middle of the biggest traffic roundabout Peter had ever seen. There were cars everywhere!

"Do you need a rest, Dad?" Margo questioned.

"I'm not tired," he protested. "I wouldn't mind a coffee though, but it will be very expensive in this street."

"Don't worry about that," Andrew reassured him. "You're paying!" Andrew was forever the joker.

As it was a nice, reasonably warm day, they sat outside and waited for a waiter to come and take their order. They were waiting when Margo noticed her father's demeanour had changed dramatically, and he was visibly shaking!

"Are you okay, Dad?" Margo asked her father.

"No, I'm not," he replied, really scaring her.

"Why? What's the matter?" she asked, very worried now.

"I think I have just seen a monster!" he stated.

"What do you mean, Dad?" Margo demanded.

"That man over there with his back to us," Peter revealed. "I think – No - I'm sure he's the man from the camp, the man they called, 'The Beast of Auschwitz.'"

"Are you sure?" Margo questioned. "Your eyes aren't what they used to be."

"No, I'm not sure," Peter answered, "but I soon will be."

He stood up and walked the five yards to the table where the man was sitting, still with his back to them. Peter hovered over the man but he did not look up.

"Heinz Kappler!" Peter announced. The man ignored him. "Heinz Kappler," Peter said again, this time more forcibly. Again, the man ignored him. "I know it's you, you snivelling Nazi bastard!" he shouted, attracting attention now from everyone sitting close by.

"You, Sir have made a mistake," the man replied. "My name is Karl Shute."

"You can change your name but I will always know who you really are, and I know you are SS Officer Heinz Kappler, the Beast of Auschwitz," Peter stated, becoming more and more incensed.

"Auschwitz, where is this place which you speak of, Auschwitz?" the older man questioned.

"You know damn well where it is," Peter instructed. "You ran the camp with Rudolph Höss and you made my life, along with the lives of millions of others a living hell!"

"You have me confused with someone else. I'm sorry," the man claimed again.

"Listen you Nazi dog, in 1947 I watched Rudolph Höss die," Peter said angrily. "I was there. I witnessed his hanging outside the Gestapo offices at Auschwitz One, and I will be there again to watch you hang!"

"Again, I tell you that you have the wrong man," the elderly man still insisted. "My name is Karl Shute."

Peter bent down and lowered himself to be head height to the man, and then whispered in his ear. "You are Heinz Kappler and I am going to see you executed for what you did to my beautiful Margo."

"Ah, lovely Margo Koval?" the man queried, before realising he'd just given himself away.

"Yes, you murdering bastard, Margo Koval, the girl I loved and the girl you murdered!" Peter was outrageously angry by now, but became even angrier when Heinz Kappler began laughing.

"Why are you laughing?" he demanded, smashing his fist down on the table and sending Kappler's coffee flying everywhere.

"If I tell you, you must promise to leave me alone to get on with the rest of my life," Kappler demanded. Peter nodded in

211

agreement, but this was not good enough for the beast. "Promise," he shouted.

"Okay, I promise," Peter said, but knew he was lying.

"Before you begin, I want to ask you something," he said, needing clarification. "When I watched you leaving the camp with the girls that day, I shouted to Margo. Did she hear me?"

"Margo – Margo – I love you Margo," Kappler laughed, taunting Peter as though he was still the young boy in the camp. "Yes, she heard you, but I ordered her to ignore you. I told them all that if ANY of the girls turned around to look at you, including Margo Koval, I would have YOU shot. So her not acknowledging your pathetic pleas actually saved your life, at least for an hour or two!" He laughed again.

"I'm warning you Kappler, I am not that young boy anymore, and you are sitting here with no gun and no Nazi or SS officers or guards to protect you. You also have no uniform to hide behind anymore, so there is nothing stopping me from knocking seven bails of shit out of you – and I could, believe me!"

"Okay Jew Boy............."

"Don't you call me that," Peter demanded, banging his fist down on the table again. "You had no rights then, and you definitely have no right to call me that now."

"Do you want to know what happened to Koval, or not?" Kappler argued, knowing that at that moment he still had the upper hand.

"Yes, I want to know what happened to my beautiful Margo that day," Peter confessed. "Tell me how she died? Did you take all the girls into the forest and shoot them all? Was she left to rot in a shallow mass grave?"

Kappler laughed again. "What is your name?" he questioned.

"It's Peter," the younger man admitted, not really believing that this monster sitting before him did not really know of his true identity.

"Well Peter," he laughed again. "Your beautiful Margo Koval, as you call her, did NOT die that day – none of them did."

"What do you mean?" Peter was confused. "You mean she's still alive?"

"I do not know the answer to that question, but all I know is, she did not die that day," Kappler stated again.

"What happened?" Peter asked the beast as he sat down to listen to the story, trying to remain a little calmer now.

"You watched as we walked out of the camp," Kappler began.

"Marched out," Peter corrected the monster.

"Okay, marched out," Kappler said angrily, appearing to have the upper hand again, just as he did back in his camp days. "Do you want to hear the story or just interrupt me?"

"Sorry," Peter apologised without knowing why.

"We marched out of the camp that day," Kappler began. "Now whatever you might think, the intention was never to execute those women that day. We'd been ordered to march them to a place called, Wodzislaw, some thirty-five miles away. There they were to be put on freight trains to be taken to various concentration camps all over Germany."

"So what happened?" an impatient Peter queried.

"We didn't make it very far at all," Kappler confessed. "We'd been going for around two hours and were walking, okay, marching along a country lane lined with trees and hedges, when we rounded a corner in the lane.

Suddenly we encountered three Russian Cossacks sitting astride three magnificent white stallions and occupying the full width of the lane. We knew the Russian Army were in the area and presumed these men were the lookout party.

Instantly every one of my men threw down their weapons and raised their hands high in the air in surrender. These Cossacks were not even holding rifles at the time, but they were holding the most enormous swords I have ever seen.

I believe my men thought that if they shot this advance party, there would quickly be three thousand Russian troops coming over the brow of the hill and they would all be slain. I don't really blame them though," Kappler admitted. "Every one of us knew we'd lost the war by then, so what was the point of them losing their lives as well?"

"I could ask you the same question about the three and a half million Jews you slaughtered. What was the point of them dying?" Peter mentioned angrily, but Kappler ignored the remark and the younger of the two continued. "So what happened to Margo?" he questioned, now even more desperate for information.

"How would I know?" Kappler laughed. "I threw myself through the hedgerow and ran for my life. I did not stop running until I reached Switzerland! For all I know, your Margo Koval was taken away by the Russians and fell in love with one of them. Maybe she married one of the three good looking Cossacks and is now a Muscovite whore!"

Peter could contain himself no longer and he slapped Kappler around the face, not too powerfully, but hard enough for it to sting.

"You disgusting Nazi bastard, you are a waste of human life!" Peter retaliated, he was furious. "So you're telling me that you know nothing to help me find Margo, so why should I not have you arrested for committing war crimes?"

"I said I do not know where she went," Kappler began, "but I do know where she came from. And if she's still alive and living in Poland, there is a good chance she returned to her home town."

"And where is that?" Peter asked.

"No - No - No – It's not that easy," Kappler stated. "This is my last piece of leverage. Before I tell you this, I want you to swear that you promise to let me stand up, walk away, and get on with the rest of my life in freedom." He looked at Peter for conformation.

"Kappler, I swear on my mother's life," he said.

"Okay then," Kappler smiled. "There is a small town in Poland where twenty-five percent of the population were Jewish. We began taking these people to work camps in 1940. At that time, there were many children not old enough to be sent for work so they were left behind. Your Margo Koval would have been one of those children. In the summer of 1943, these 'children' had reached the age when they could be sent to a camp, so they were rounded up and transported to Auschwitz Birkenau.

I remember the day she arrived. She was beautiful then and I selected her to work and not to die. You see, Jew Boy, I saved her life for you. You should be thanking me."

"So what's the name of that town?" Peter asked, now on the edge of his seat.

"Promise," Kappler demanded.

""I promise," Peter said once again.

"It's a town called, Tarnow," Kappler divulged.

"Tarnow?" Peter questioned looking for conformation.

"Yes, Tarnow," Heinz Kappler confirmed.

Instantly Peter jumped to his feet. "Andrew, come here quickly," he shouted to his son in law. Andrew rushed to his aid. "Hold this bastard piece of shit while I fetch the police. He is a war criminal and needs to be brought to justice."

"You promised," Kappler demanded looking at Peter with distain, as rugby playing Andrew had him pinned down to the chair. "You swore on your mother's life!" he said again.

"Yes I did," Peter agreed. "But you sent her to the gas chamber in October 1943!"

It was now Peter's turn to gloat, laughing as he ran inside the café to phone for, 'The Police Nationale' to come and arrest this beast.

They were there in seconds, and after hearing what Heinz Kappler was, a war criminal, he was bundled unceremoniously into the back of the car and taken away. Peter travelled in another car to the station, where he gave a very long and detailed statement.

That evening, when he arrived back at the Hotel de Paris, the family were waiting for him. When he told them the full story about the man he'd had arrested, he realised he would have to tell his daughter the truth about his love for Margo, the first girl he'd ever loved, but he had nothing to worry about.

"So her name was Margo Koval?" his daughter asked.

"Yes it was, and I hope it still is," Peter stated.

"So you had me named after the girl from the camp?" Margo questioned.

"Yes, I'm sorry sweetheart," Peter said.

"Don't apologise, Dad, I am highly honoured to be named after someone who experienced Auschwitz Birkenau with you," his daughter told him. "Did Mum know about her?"

"No darling, I never told her," Peter confessed.

"You were so young when you lost her, Dad," Margo said. "It must have been heartbreaking for you. Did you love her?"

"Yes, I loved her," Peter admitted, but then quickly added. "But it never stopped me from loving your mother."

"I know that, Dad. I always knew you and Mum loved each other. But to have kept this other Margo secret from her must have been heartbreaking for you."

"It was, but I always had to remain faithful to your mum," Peter revealed. "I always wanted to be faithful to your mum because I loved her so very much."

"But Mum's gone now, Dad, and you've been alone for long enough," Margo said, which surprised him.

"What are you saying?" Peter asked his daughter.

"I'm saying go now Dad, go and look for her," his daughter, Margo insisted.

Do you mean it?" he questioned.

"Yes Dad, go and find your first love," she told him. "Go now and find her – Go and find your beautiful Margo Koval."

# CHAPTER 23
# RETURN TO POLAND

The plane touched down on the runway of 'Krakow Balice Airport' in the mid afternoon of Thursday the 26th of May 1977. Leaving the arrivals after collecting his luggage, Peter made his way outside to the taxi rank, where he took a taxi to the centre of Krakow, which was a short six mile journey.

That morning he'd left the rest of his family at the airport outside Paris, the Paris Charles de Gaulle. Following the events of the meeting with Kappler, he'd decided to stay for the duration of the five day holiday. He'd made a promise to babysit for little Grace so her parents could enjoy the romance of the city, and he kept to his promise so as not to spoil their vacation.

As he'd said to Margo and Andrew, "I have waited thirty-two years to find her, so three more days will not make any great difference."

In the heat of the moment, what Peter hadn't realised about that day when he'd ran into Heinz Kappler in Paris, was the fact that it was actually the day of his fiftieth birthday. He decided that meeting Kappler and having him arrested that day, was possibly the best birthday present he'd ever received!

He had the taxi drop him off at his old hunting ground, the Main Square in the old town. On first impressions, it looked as though time had stood still and nothing had changed, but when about to enter the café where he'd worked all those years ago, he found it was now a Starbucks and full of tourists.

He thought about walking to the Ratusz, but he decided that his friend, Mr. Nowak, must have long since retired so decided against it. Instead, he went to one of the more conventional cafés and ordered a 'Café Americano,' forgetting just how damn strong the coffee was in this country.

He introduced himself to the barista, and after telling him a brief history about his life, and what he was doing here, he asked the young man for directions to Tarnow.

"How far is it from Krakow?" he questioned the young barista.

"By road, Sir, it would be about a fifty to sixty mile drive," the young man instructed, as he went to fetch a map.

Peter couldn't believe it. If he does find Margo alive and living in Tarnow, then all those years ago, for all that time, pain and longing, she was only less than sixty miles away!

The young man returned with a map and Peter studied it, deciding the drive was straight forward. All he needed was a car. He remedied this problem by going to the local Hertz office and rented a 'Syrena,' not the biggest or the most comfortable car, but it would do the job he needed.

Two hours later, he checked into a hotel in the centre of Tarnow. He thought he'd relax that evening and then begin the search in the morning. However, in all his excitement, sleep evaded him.

The next day, Friday, he woke bright, and early. He had eventually fallen into a deep sleep around three, but was wide awake again by six. After taking breakfast in the hotel, he ventured into the sunshine of the day to begin his search.

He thought about how he was going to proceed. How was he going to find her? He had no photo to show people, and maybe she had a different surname by now.

Suddenly he had a brilliant idea. Instead of asking strangers, "Have you seen this girl?" he had another question for them. He rolled up his left sleeve to reveal the Two-Nine-Eight-Six-One tattoo. He then asked them, "Excuse me, I'm sorry to bother you, but do you know anyone else in this town that has numbers tattooed on their left arm like this?" He did not say, "Do you know any ladies," as he thought that maybe someone would know a man with a tattoo. If so, this man might know of Margo and her whereabouts.

Although he thought it a brilliant idea, after the one hundredth person answered with a negative and blank stare, he wondered if he'd ever find her. He was given one piece of advice, however, when one man told him where in the town he thought she might be, if still alive.

"You need to go to the Old Town," he told Peter, "If your friend is still living here in Tarnow, that's the place where she'll be. It's not far from an old Jewish cemetery. The shame is that it was destroyed by the Germans in the war, with many Jews being shot there during the occupation.

There's a monument there now at the entrance to where the cemetery once stood. Find the monument and you will have found the correct area to look. Good luck, my friend," the man said, extending his arm to shake Peter's hand.

"Thank you, Sir," Peter said, thanking the man in return and then adding. "And may God be with you."

"And with you," the gent replied. "I hope you find your girl."

Rejuvenated by this encounter, Peter continued his search with renewed vigour. One hour later, he found the monument. He was now in the right area and asked a few more people the same question he'd been asking all morning.

"Excuse me," he'd ask politely. "Have you seen anyone with a number like this on their arm?"

After asking twenty more people and getting the same, "No, Sorry" reply, Peter decided it was time for a break, so headed towards the nearest café for a coffee and a sandwich.

After sitting at a table a waiter came to take his order, a ham and cheese sandwich and a cola with ice and lemon. When the waiter returned, Peter asked him the same question he'd been asking all morning. However, this time, instead of just saying "No," the waiter asked why he was asking. Peter gave him the reason and the young man turned to the crowded café.

"Excuse me everyone, could I have your full attention please?" As he said this, at least thirty people turned to face him. "This gentleman has a question for you all," he told the audience, gesturing for Peter to stand and address them. Peter stood to face the gathering.

"Thank you everyone. I am looking for an old friend whom I have not seen for thirty-two years. We were together at Auschwitz Birkenau from nineteen forty-three until nineteen forty-five, but we were cruelly separated on our final day in the camp.

Her name then was Margo Koval and she has a number tattooed on her left arm, just like this." He raised his left arm and revealed the Two-Nine-Eight-Six-One tattoo. "Have any of you seen anyone with a tattoo like this."

"I have," Peter heard a voice say. He turned to the direction it came from, and saw it was a young man of about seventeen years of age.

"You have seen this lady?" Peter questioned frantically.

"I don't know anything about Auschwitz, nor do I know anyone by that name of Margo Koval," he said, giving Peter a sinking feeling, but then the youngster continued. "But I do know of a lady with numbers on her arm."

"How do you know her?" Peter asked, desperate now for information.

"I don't know her," the young man replied, "but I remember a lady serving me in the cake shop. I remember her sleeve riding up and she became embarrassed when I spotted the numbers on her arm. I didn't realise it was a tattoo, but thought she'd written it on her arm herself. I thought it might be a phone number or something."

"Where is this shop?" Peter asked, almost bursting with excitement by now.

It's really close, only five streets from here," the young man smiled whilst drawing him a map.

"Thank you – Thank you – Thank you," Peter kept repeating, over, and over again!

Twenty minutes later, Peter stood outside a shop where both bread and cakes were on sale. He was nervous! This was probably the most nervous he'd ever been in his life, and that included the night he'd arrived at Auschwitz Birkenau.

He wasn't nervous about walking inside and finding Margo, he was worried about going inside and it not being her. If this were the case, then everything he'd dreamed about for all these years would be lost and gone forever. Finally, he plucked up the courage to find out the truth and headed towards the building.

As he entered the shop, a bell above the door rang as it opened and it sounded again when it closed behind him. Peter stood there and noticed a woman behind the counter with her back to him. She was arranging some cakes on a display stand.

"Just a minute," she said.

Peter looked at her. She was a little plumper than the Margo he'd known in the camp, and the blonde hair was shorter and not so shiny, with a little grey coming through.

He couldn't be sure if it was her or not, but then she turned around to face him.

"Can I help...?" she began, but stopped mid sentence.

The skin was older and not so tight, but when he saw her smile, he was quite sure. Then he saw her eyes and he was certain. They were the same beautiful, piercing blue eyes that sparkled like cool pools of water. These were the same eyes that he'd fallen in love with, on that first day when he'd seen her in Kanada Sorting Room 10.

He looked at her and her face contorted as she stared back and studied him.

Was it him, could it be him?

Suddenly she could contain herself no longer, as she realized whom it was standing before her.

"PETER!" she screamed.

"MARGO!" he yelled.

"Peter is that really you?" She was ecstatic.

"YES – Yes Margo. It's really me," he shouted at her.

Margo dropped an entire tray of cakes that she'd been holding and ran as fast as she could from behind the counter. When she reached Peter, she threw herself at him, almost knocking him to the floor.

"Peter, I never thought I would ever see you again. I thought you were dead," she cried, kissing him over, and over again.

"I too thought you were dead, Margo. I thought they'd shot you that day when I watched you leave the camp," Peter admitted. "But I have never given up looking for you, and now, here you are."

"Oh Peter, I have never stopped loving you," Margo confessed. "Just lately I have been praying for something good to happen in my life, and today my prayers have been answered. I cannot believe this. But how on earth did you find me?"

"Margo, you will never believe me when I tell you," he replied.

Her boss told her to finish work immediately and go with Peter. He thanked the boss and said to Margo, "Come on. I want to take you somewhere."

"Now?" she questioned.

"Yes, right now," Peter replied, and Margo could see he was excited. Although she was confused, after all these years apart she would follow him anywhere.

Peter looked extremely proud as he walked hand in hand with Margo through the streets of the town. Eventually they arrived at the same café where Peter had been given the information to find her.

They entered, and when reaching the serving counter, Peter turned to face the customers, many of whom were still there from earlier.

"Ladies and Gentlemen," he began, confusing his companion, "I give you the very beautiful, Margo Koval. After all this time I have finally found the girl I fell in love with many years ago – and here she is."

Everyone in the café stood from their tables and began applauding in unison. The clapping went on for a long time but reached a crescendo when Peter took Margo in his arms and kissed her, and it was not an Auschwitz peck on the cheek; this was a full blown, lip tingling smacker. Everyone in the place wanted to come and shake their hands, personally giving them all their best wishes for the future.

The young barista looked at Peter seriously and said, "Peter, you have found her. I am so very pleased for you, but please, do not lose her again!"

"Never," Peter shouted. "Now, drinks for everyone," Peter shouted, and received yet more rapturous applause and cheering.

They sat at the table and told each other their life stories, all the time holding hands. Peter told her about what happened that day and how he'd escaped.

He told her about Paul Fuster sparing his life, and how he was lucky to have been found and then taken in by Rubin and

224

Steph, especially his being found by the sharp end of Rubin's pitch fork!

"Did you ever marry, Peter?" she asked, surprising him with her bluntness.

"Yes. I'm sorry Margo," he stated. "I did."

"Sorry?" she queried. "Sorry for what? You have nothing to be sorry about, you didn't know if I was dead or alive, and you deserved a happy life. Did you have a happy life? Please tell me you had a happy life."

"Yes, I had a happy life, and my wife was a wonderful woman," he admitted. "But every day I was with Jayne, I felt guilty for being unfaithful to you and your memory."

Hearing this brought tears to Margo's eyes, but when she heard about his daughter, she was reduced to a blubbering mess.

"You named your daughter after me?" she cried. "That's wonderful. Thank you. I hope one day I can meet her, does she know about me?"

She does now," Peter revealed, "but only since the past few days."

"Only a few days?" she questioned. "Why. What happened?"

"You will not believe what happened last Monday," he said.

He then told her about the events in Paris. She flinched when hearing Heinz Kappler's name. Like Peter, she also thought Kappler was dead, but when Peter told her about him telling him where to look for 'Lovely Margo,' she was actually thankful to the Beast!

"At last he did something good in his life," she observed.

"Yes, just before the French Police came when I had them arrest him!" Peter informed her, and Margo smiled at him in admiration. She thought he was such a brave man to have confronted that terrible monster!

"Margo, did you ever marry?" Peter asked his darling.

"No I never did," Margo replied. "The truth is that I never found any man whom I loved as much as you."

Margo asked him how he'd met his wife, and she smiled as he recollected that happy evening when he'd met Jayne at the funfair.

"You caught her when she fell from the carousel?" Margo laughed. "Your wife was a very clever girl."

"Why do you say that?" he questioned.

"Oh Peter, you don't really think that was an accident when she fell into your arms," Margo laughed. "She planned it Peter. I bet she watched you from that carousel horse and liked what she saw. She waited for you to be in position and then she stumbled – just enough for you to notice and come rushing to her aid." She laughed again. He loved seeing how happy she was.

Peter was saddened to hear that Margo had never married because she never considered any man worthy of her company when compared to him. The result of this was that she'd had a sad and lonely life, but he intended to change all that.

"Margo," he said, "When we were together in the camp, there was something I always wanted to do with you. I daydreamed about it every day and hoped I would dream about it when I finally drifted off to sleep."

"What's that, Peter," she asked, but looked concerned.

"Every day I dreamed that the war would end and we'd be rescued. It was always my dream to walk out of the camp holding hands with you, but Kappler deprived me of my dream."

"How I hated that man," Margo responded."

Would you go back with me and make my dream come true?" Peter asked.

"Go back to the camp?" she asked, looking nervous.

"Yes, back to Auschwitz Birkenau," he replied.

"I will," she said after a few moments whilst deep in thought. "But only if you promise to hold me very, very tightly."

"Margo, I promise to hold you very tightly for the rest of my life. Return with me to the camp and I promise to squeeze every last breath of air from your lungs," he laughed. He could not remember the last time he'd been this happy.

Margo came with him while he checked out of his hotel and they drove together to her apartment on the outskirts of the city. It was nothing fancy, but she said it was silly to pay hotel prices when she had a perfectly good place where he could stay for nothing.

Without knowing anything about his new life or his wealth, Peter loved the idea that Margo loved him for who he was. She had no idea of how wealthy he'd become.

They chatted well into the night. It was as though the past thirty-two years had never happened and they were two teenagers again, two teenagers who were obviously still madly in love.

The next morning they set off for the ninety mile drive to the camp, but first, Peter made an announcement.

"Margo, I want to take you somewhere on the way," he said. "There are some very important people I want you to meet."

She agreed and he headed for Krakow. It was silly, but he only knew how to get to the farm when driving from the city, so he drove that way so he wouldn't get lost and look stupid.

After driving through the city and leaving it behind, he reached the more familiar county lanes and noticed one house by the roadside that looked familiar. He stopped the car to take a closer look.

It was the little house where they'd seen the old couple selling their rotten vegetables, all those years ago. He smiled as he recollected that day. The table was gone from outside the door and the old couple must have been long gone. The house looked freshly painted and there was a little white picket fence separating the garden from the dangers of the road.

Peter smiled as he saw a small boy and girl playing in the garden. 'New life,' he thought.

"Why are you smiling, Peter," Margo asked, and he told her about that day when Rubin had driven him to Krakow and they'd stopped to help the old couple.

"Why were you going to Krakow that day," she questioned.

"To search for you," he revealed. His reply made her happy and she rewarded him with a kiss.

An hour later, they drove through the gate to the farm. It looked very different from the last time he'd seen this place. There were now many cows grazing on the lush grass, the barn which had been his first resting place was now larger than before, and there was now a large chicken coup built on one side of it.

Peter was pleased to see that the house had remained the same, as did the figures of the two people who emerged from the door to greet them, older, but just as welcoming.

"Steph – Rubin – It's so wonderful to see you," Peter said.

"Rubin," Steph shouted, "Our son has come home!" She was very excited to see Peter, but then turned her attention to his travelling companion. "You must be Margo. Come here child."

"You know about me?" Margo questioned.

"Of course, Peter never stopped talking about you in all the time he stayed here with us," Steph informed her. "Now, come here." She opened her arms, inviting Margo into an embrace. Margo willingly accepted the hug and enjoyed the experience of having Steph's big strong arms wrapped around her.

"It's been a long time since anyone called me child," Margo laughed.

"To me, your Peter will always be the young man who came here in nineteen forty-five, and he will always be our son," Steph told a grateful Margo.

"And now we have a daughter," Rubin added. "Mother, meet our daughter, Margo."

"I'm honoured to meet you both," Margo announced, bursting with pride at how they'd accepted her into their family group.

They went inside the house and Peter was relieved to find it was exactly the same as he'd known before. It still had the same furniture and magnificent open wood fire, although it was too hot to light today. The younger man thought it was like entering a time-capsule.

"Sit down, child," Steph invited Margo, who immediately sat herself upon an old wooden rocking chair. Steph began to laugh and Margo looked at her inquisitively.

"Thirty-two years ago, Peter sat in that exact chair," Steph explained. "He told us all about his life in Auschwitz Birkenau, but all the time he told us, he remained strong."

Margo looked at Peter admiringly, as Steph continued. "But then he told us about a girl he'd met in the camp, a girl called Margo Koval. He told us how much he loved her and

229

how he'd lost her the day before arriving here. He sat in that chair and cried his eyes out. He also told us that he would never stop looking for you, and now you are here. You're here with us. He's found you, and it's wonderful."

By now, Margo had tears in her eyes. It had been such a very long time since she'd felt this loved.

They discussed their intentions to go and visit Auschwitz. Although Rubin and Steph couldn't understand why they wanted to do this, they respected the decision and thought there must have been a good reason, but Rubin made a suggestion.

"Look you two, you have only just arrived and we have lots of catching up to do," he said, and then made a suggestion. "Auschwitz is going nowhere. It will still be there tomorrow, so why don't you stay here tonight?"

"Careful Margo," Peter said jokingly," he wants to wake you with his pitchfork!" Everyone laughed at this insinuation.

"Do you still have the pitchfork?" Margo questioned.

"It's in pride of place," Rubin smiled.

The next morning, after one of Steph's famous Polish breakfasts with specially made freshly baked bread, the four gathered outside Peter's hire car to say their goodbyes. As Rubin hugged Margo and Peter squeezed Steph as tightly as he could, he whispered something in her ear. When they swapped 'hug partners,' as Steph cuddled Margo, the younger of the two began to cry.

"Steph, it has been so wonderful to meet you and Rubin. Just think, four days ago I didn't even know you existed, but now you are my family," Margo said, bringing a lump to the older woman's throat. "Thank you so much for taking care of Peter all those years ago. He was so lucky to find you."

"Thank you darling," Steph replied. "It was our pleasure to take care of that lovely young man, but now it's your turn to take care of our Peter, and I know you will. It's very obvious how much you two love each other."

"In all those years apart, I never stopped loving him," Margo admitted.

"I know, sweetheart," Steph replied. "I know."

As the car containing Peter and Margo pulled away, Rubin asked his wife why she was not sad.

"What did Peter say to you?" he questioned his wife.

"He told me that we will see him and Margo again," Steph confirmed. "He said we will see them again, and we will see them very soon."

# CHAPTER 24
# CROSSING THE LINE

The building loomed close and Margo could feel the tension building inside her. All the memories of being interred in here came flooding back, all the death, the smell of disease, the putrid black smoke coming from the chimneys, the human skeletons walking around, and for what? What did all that pain and suffering actually achieve? It achieved nothing!

She couldn't believe there were actually now tourists visiting the camp and milling about the place by choice, although she understood why when Peter told her they were paying their respects to all the casualties of the holocaust.

"The authorities wanted to keep Auschwitz and Auschwitz Birkenau open to the public, so it would remind them that what happened before in the forties, the holocaust, should never be repeated. It must never happen again," Peter told an attentive Margo.

After parking the car, they walked towards Auschwitz Camp One, the first camp. Peter thought he would ease her in gently by going to the place where nothing actually happened to them, before persuading her to go to 'their' camp.

Walking around the place, Peter remembered his last visit here in 1947, noting that it looked exactly the same in every way. Margo gripped his hand, almost squeezing the blood from it as she remembered the times she'd come here when waitressing at 'The Retreat.'

When they came to Block 24, the old brothel where Margo washed and put on a clean waitressing uniform, Peter made a confession.

"Margo, when I came here thirty years ago, I touched this door," he told her.

"Why?" she queried most intrigued.

"I touched the door because I knew you'd walked through it a few times. By touching it, it made me feel close to you," he confessed.

Margo gave him one of those smiles that had made him fall in love with her all those years ago, during those dark, desperate times.

Continuing to walk around the camp, they encountered a group of people currently being spoken to by a tour guide. They listened to what the young girl was telling them, but Margo became angry by what the girl was saying.

"She's glamorising it, Peter," she stressed. "She makes it sound like this was a holiday camp, a place to be enjoyed!"

The tour guide heard what Margo had said and apologised for making light of the camp.

"Of course none of us know what it was really like to have been here during the war," she said.

"How old are you?" Margo questioned the young guide.

"I am seventeen," she revealed. "I'm doing this work during my school holidays."

"Well let me tell you something," Margo began. "When I was your age, I'd already been in Auschwitz Birkenau for more than a year, and it was certainly no holiday camp, I can tell you!"

Margo rolled up her left sleeve and showed all the visitors her Two-Three-Three-One-Two tattoo. "This is how those bastards treated us. They took every last piece of dignity away from us, even taking our names away!"

This was the first time that Peter had ever seen Margo angry, although God knows she had plenty to be angry about during her time spent in this evil place.

"I'm very sorry," the young girl told Margo.

She then asked if they might answer a few questions from the visitors, or tell them more about their stories of life in the camp.

Peter and Margo, now a lot calmer and able to forgive the young girl's stupidity, were happy to do this and answer these questions for fifteen minutes or so.

The group listened intently to stories of their time spent in this place, both good and bad, but mostly bad. They gasped when it was revealed to the group about how SS officer Heinz Kappler had 'introduced' them to each other, and they marvelled at the story of Peter's escape, and how he owed his life to another SS officer, Paul Fuster.

Peter did not tell them about the twelve Hungarian prisoners who were shot as they lay face down in the mud at the morning roll call, he thought that might be a little too graphic for them.

In the end, the young tour guide thanked them both, and then all was forgiven, with Margo giving the youngster a nice hug. In return, the young girl promised she would do more research about the camp history, so she could tell the visitors the real story in the future.

Margo and Peter walked on and eventually reached the spot where thirty years previously, as a younger man he'd witnessed the hanging of Rudolph Höss. Strangely, Peter began to laugh.

"What do you find so amusing?" Margo questioned. "Why are you laughing?"

"I'm sorry, but it's funny," he replied, pointing to the building where Höss was imprisoned before being taken to the gallows.

"You see that building?" Peter asked Margo. "Well that was the Gestapo office where they interrogated and tortured prisoners, sometimes to death."

"So what's funny?" Margo asked again.

"Look at it now," Peter shouted. "They have turned it into the public toilets. That has to be the ultimate insult to those murdering Gestapo bastards!"

He found the conversion of the Gestapo HQ into public toilets to be most amusing. However, one thing he didn't understand was that the 'temporary gallows' built to execute Rudolph Höss in 1947 were still standing.

"Why did you come to watch that man being hanged?" Margo asked, feeling a little concerned.

"Margo, I didn't come to watch him being executed," Peter revealed. "I came to see if you were here, or if anyone was here who knew you."

"Oh Peter, I don't believe it," Margo confessed. "I heard about that day and was told I could have gone, but I didn't think I could watch that evil man die. If I'd gone that day we would have met, and all those wasted years would never have happened."

"Don't worry, my Angel, we're here now, reunited and together again," he smiled at his girl, reassuring her. He then said something profound when he said, "Margo, we cannot change the past, but we can change the future."

He took her in his arms and kissed her, and the years seemed to gently roll away.

The two left Auschwitz Camp One arm in arm. After leaving the hire car parked in the car park, they caught the free tourist bus to Auschwitz Birkenau.

Peter could see that Margo was now starting to get very nervous, so he put his arm around her. "Don't worry, I will take good care of you my darling," he said, trying to calm her even more.

As they stood at the huge archway entrance, Margo began to physically shake.

"Come on sweetheart, come with me," Peter said. "There is no one here now to do you any harm, the ghosts have all gone. I will never let anyone harm you ever again."

They were just about to cross the line at the entrance, the imaginary line where one step means you have crossed into the 'dark side,' when Peter let go of her hand.

"What's the matter, Peter? You don't want to hold my hand?" she questioned, looking hurt.

"No, it's not that. My dream was never to walk 'into' the camp holding your hand; it was always to hold your hand when walking out," he said. "Please Margo, just walk through the entrance, take a few steps alone, and then I can hold your hand again."

She did as Peter requested, and as soon as she was across the imaginary line and was inside, Peter took her back in his arms and kissed her.

"Margo," he said, "do you realise that that was our first real kiss inside Auschwitz Birkenau?" Hearing him say this made her smile.

She stared at the Kanada building and the memories came flooding back, mostly bad, but she had to admit that some were also good, like the day when she'd met Peter for the first time, when their eyes met across a crowded room.

Who would have known then that, thirty-four years after that meeting they'd be back here again, but this time by choice and not at gunpoint?

Margo looked up at the watchtower. "It's so strange being in here without a machine gun being pointed at you," she remarked. Peter smiled and answered with a hug.

Unfortunately the ladder which Peter had climbed to get into the tower in 1947 had long since been taken away, so there was no access possible anymore. This made him a little upset, because he wanted to take Margo up there so she could see the immense size of the place, as he'd done on his last visit.

They continued to walk inside the camp and found the remnants of Hut 27, where Peter bowed his head in the memory of Franz, the man who welcomed and helped him on the night he'd arrived on the transport.

Sadly, Hut 44, the gypsy hut where the party had taken place during Christmas 1943 was no longer standing, long since demolished, along with many other huts.

Peter noticed that there was one hut standing that had been restored to its former glory, in an attempt to make it look just like it did when Peter and Margo were there. Stepping inside, the pair were transported back to those heady times.

They both couldn't believe how they'd survived these cramped, overcrowded conditions, but were also angry that this hut had been thoroughly cleansed and sanitised, so the visitors would have no idea of how dirty, smelly and lice ridden the place would have been during the times of capture.

The final area they visited was the main square, the place where they used to spend Sunday afternoons listening to the camp orchestra playing classical music. They remembered how they secretly stroked the back of each other's hand, all the time trying not to be seen showing affection for each other in case the guards spotted them.

"I always wanted to do this," Peter announced.

"What?" Margo questioned.

"This!" Having said this, he grabbed her, took her in his arms and planted a big kiss on her lips. She in turn offered no resistance.

"Peter, can we go now?" Margo asked him.

"Of course," he replied. However, she was surprised to see that he was getting nervous now.

"What's wrong?" she questioned.

"Nothing," he lied. Inside he was as nervous as hell!

When they were five yards from the entrance, although this time it was the exit to the camp, Peter stopped.

"Can we take this slowly," he said. "I have been dreaming about this moment for a very long time and want to savour every second of it, walking out of the camp holding your hand."

She smiled at him, but could still see he was nervous about something. "Okay Peter Florea," she smiled, now giving him courage. "Whenever you're ready," she announced.

He held out his hand, which she took willingly, and they walked at a snail's pace to the imaginary line between being inside the camp and the outside world. When they reached the exact spot, he suddenly stopped, turned to face her, and dropped to his knee.

"Margo, I lost you once and I never want to lose you again," he began.

"Peter?" she queried. "What's going on? Why are you down there?"

"Margo Koval, would you do me the honour of making me the happiest man alive?" he asked, now also visibly shaking, as she had done before.

"Peter, what are you saying?" a confused Margo questioned.

"What I am saying is, "Peter began. "Margo Koval, will you do me the honour of becoming my wife? Will you marry me?"

"YES!" she screamed. "Peter, of course I'll marry you."

# EPILOGUE

After Peter had him arrested, Heinz Kappler was taken from Paris and transported to Berlin, where he was put on trial for war crimes including murder, as well as crimes against humanity. His trial began in August 1977.

With the help of Peter's evidence, he was found guilty and sentenced to death. However, by then the death penalty had long since been abolished, so his sentence was changed to life in prison. With no chance of ever being released, he would die behind bars. He began his sentence in Spandau Prison, the prison located in the Spandau region of western Berlin.

At the time of his sentence, he was sixty-six years of age and had already enjoyed thirty-two years more life and freedom than most of the guards of whom he'd been in charge. He died in his Spandau cell in 1986 aged seventy-five.

Whilst in the prison he befriended another member of the Nazi party, Adolph Hitler's right hand man, Rudolph Hess, not to be confused with Rudolph Höss, the man hanged at Auschwitz, an act witnessed by Peter in 1947.

During the war years, Rudolph Hess was the one man Heinz Kappler feared, however, in Spandau, the two became good friends, or as good as they were allowed to become.

One year after the death of Heinz Kappler, Rudolph Hess died in his cell. It was believed at the time that he'd taken his own life, but this was never proved. It was Monday the 17th of August 1987 when his guards found him dead in his cell. He was ninety-three years of age when he passed.

Later that year, Spandau Prison was demolished. The authorities worried it could become a shrine for Nazi sympathisers, so it was demolished for this reason. In the place where it once stood now stands a shopping centre.

Paul Fuster was originally tried as part of a group of ten SS officers from Auschwitz Birkenau. All ten were found guilty of murder and crimes against humanity and were all sentenced to be executed by hanging.

However, thanks partly to Peter's letter, as well as other ex prisoners coming forward in support of him, his defence team were able to get his sentence reduced to five years prison, but suspended for twenty-four months. He walked out of the trial that day as a free man.

Paul Fuster moved back to his home town of Peina and continued his university studies at Hannover. He qualified with a degree in law and became one of the country's top lawyers.

He never forgot his days in Auschwitz Birkenau and because of his time there, he made a career out of always representing the 'underdog,' the poor people who couldn't normally afford good representation. This was, of course, as long as he was one hundred percent sure they were innocent.

Paul Fuster and Peter Florea never met again, which was a shame. Although both coming from different worlds, they each had something in common with the other. They had both saved each other's life.

When Heinz Kappler left the house for the camp on the morning of the 25th of January 1945, he said goodbye to his wife and children. He never returned and that was the last time they ever saw him.

Christa Kappler was discovered by the Russian liberators of Auschwitz a few days later. At first, she and the children were put under arrest, but it soon became apparent that she was an innocent party and totally oblivious to the goings on at the camp. To establish this, she was taken to Auschwitz Birkenau and was horrified to see hundreds of emaciated bodies lying around the place.

The Russians decided there was no way she could have feigned her reaction, so decided that she should be helped and not punished.

She eventually arrived back in Munich, where two years later she met and fell in love with a Canadian soldier. In 1948 she was granted a divorce from Heinz Kappler on the grounds of his desertion or possible death. Within weeks of the divorce, she and the Canadian were married and moved to Vancouver.

The names of the children were legally changed. Adolph became Adam, whilst Eva became Edith. Christa, or Christine as she became, was also very happy and relieved to lose her surname of Kappler.

Along with her Canadian husband, she had a very happy life in Vancouver. Heinz Kappler's name was never mentioned again.

William Straus and Claus Hoffer, Peter's friends in Kanada at Auschwitz Birkenau were identified as being two of the party of prisoners whom Peter had heard being mowed down by the machine gun fire, after he'd escaped from the train. This made him realise how lucky he was that day, and how close as a young man he'd come to dying – twice!

Peter brought Margo to live with him in his home city of Bath, a place he'd now called home for thirty years or more.

They were married in a church at the bottom of Bathwick Hill with a wonderful wedding reception following at The Pump Rooms, a part of the Roman Baths, with the entrance being in the Bath Abbey churchyard.

The date of the wedding was the 25<sup>th</sup> of January 1978 – Exactly thirty-three years to the day when Peter had watched Margo being marched out of the camp by Heinz Kappler. The day when he thought, he would never see her again.

Peter had Rubin and Steph flown over from Poland, the first time either of them had ever been on an airplane. Rubin was extremely proud and honoured to walk Margo down the aisle and give her away, whilst Steph was equally proud to be Margo's, 'Maid of Honour.'

Tom sent his best wishes to the happy couple, but as he said, "Somebody has to stay home and look after the farm, and of course keep the vegetable soup hot."

Sadly, the day when Peter took Rubin and Steph back to Bristol International Airport; it would be the last time they would ever be in each other's company.

Five years later, after a short illness, Rubin passed away in his sleep, followed two years later by Steph, who after losing Rubin, basically died of a broken heart. They were both in their late seventies when passing.

Tom had a priest come to the farm and consecrate a piece of land in the top field. There, side by side, they were both laid to rest. This plot was the only place on the land with a view of every inch of the farm. Tom often joked with Peter during their regular phone calls, saying, "Even in death, the old man is still watching my every move. He's probably complaining to mum, telling her, 'He's not doing that right!"

Peter and Margo returned to the land of her birth to attend the two funerals, but it would be the last time they ever set foot on Polish soil.

The day of the wedding was the start of a wonderful marriage for Peter and Margo – Mr. And Mrs. Florea.

Margo loved her new name just as much as Jayne had done all those years ago, and was proud to be the wife of Peter after all those years apart, all those long wasted years. She wished it could have been 1945, but at least it had finally happened.

Peter took early retirement so he could spend every hour of his day by Margo's side. After losing her for thirty-two years, he didn't want to waste another second of life without her.

History was repeated when he gave the jewellery shop, still named 'Samuel's High Class Jewellers,' to his daughter, Margo, and her husband, Andrew. They moved into the business premises in Abbey Green with little Grace, whilst Peter and Margo moved to the house in Lansdown, where they lived happily for many years. All those years ago when he'd decided not to sell this house, he now realised that this must have been the reason.

Margo loved her life in England and being a part of Peter's family, which was now 'her' family. She loved living in the city of Bath and sometimes pinched herself to think that she was actually a resident of this wonderful city.

If she loved her life here, the family all quickly fell in love with her. Little Grace, who'd never really known Jayne, almost instantly began calling her Granny, which Margo adored.

Peter's daughter, Margo, surprised her one day when she asked, "Margo, can I call you Mum?" Margo burst into tears and the two Margo's hugged each other for a very long time. Life could not have been better.

On the 25th of January 2003, Peter and Margo celebrated their 25th Wedding Anniversary. It had been fifty-eight years since their separation at Auschwitz Birkenau and Peter had now reached the ripe old age of seventy-six. Sadly, he was no longer in the best of health.

Two years later, at the age of seventy-eight, Peter was rushed to the Royal United Hospital in Bath with a mystery illness. Two days later, he died in Margo's arms.

The last thing he ever said to her was, "Thank you for making my life complete. I will always love you." He then smiled at her, held her hand, and quietly slipped away.

Life was never the same for Margo after this. Although the family rallied round to give her all the love they could, she never felt truly happy again. Two years after Peter's passing, she joined him. She died aged seventy-nine.

Years earlier, they'd bought a double plot at Haycombe Cemetery, where in July 2007 she was laid to rest next to the man she'd always adored since the first day she set eyes on him in Kanada. Although she'd always hated the man, she'd secretly thanked Heinz Kappler for introducing them in that strange and cruel way he had.

Peter and Margo were again reunited in a double grave on the south side of the cemetery. Peter had chosen the plot because it had beautiful views all over the rolling hills of the Mendips. On a warm summer day, there was no better place to be. The family often came to visit and sit with them, all the time enjoying the spectacular views.

On the day of her funeral, Margo's name was added to the headstone. It now read –

Here lies Margo and Peter Florea
Separated at Auschwitz
Reunited for all eternity

Thank you for reading their story

**THE END**

**Also by this author –**

# THE SECRET JEW
# OF
# MUNICH
By
## Kevin Paul Woodrow

There was a knock on the door of the apartment. She looked through the spyglass to see two Gestapo officers standing there. What did they want, had they come for her? Had she been discovered after all this time? Was she about to lose everything, including her life?

Rebecca was a beautiful teenager with many friends who loved her. However, for her, life as a young Austrian woman would change dramatically when her country was invaded by the Nazis, resulting in Austria being annexed on the 1th of March 1938.

The problem for Rebecca was that even though her family were not at all religious, her papers contained the word "Juden." This word alone was enough to make her life impossible, for in the eyes of the Nazis, as a Jew, she was the enemy.

Her friends rallied, all wanting to help. Her best friend was an artist and he made fake papers for her by copying those of another friend, but the two girls could not live in the same city, Vienna.

For this reason, Rebecca moves to live with her friend's relations, in of all places, Munich, the birth place of the Nazis. Here she will spend the entire war years hiding from the Nazis by living amongst them whilst working and socialising with them – all the time hiding in plain sight!

## THE SECRET JEW
## OF
## MUNICH
### By
### Kevin Paul Woodrow

Available from your local Amazon site
In both
EBook and Paperback

Printed in Great Britain
by Amazon

28457873R00139